SWEPT AWAY

BY
DAWN ATKINS

MILLS & BOON®
Pure reading pleasure

*First published in Great Britain 2008
by Harlequin Mills & Boon Limited,
Eton House, 18-24 Paradise Road, Richmond, Surrey TW9 1SR*

ISBN: 978 0 263 86211 9

14-0608

*Harlequin Mills & Boon policy is to use papers that are
natural, renewable and recyclable products and made from
wood grown in sustainable forests. The logging and
manufacturing processes conform to the legal environmental
regulations of the country of origin.*

*Printed and bound in Spain
by Litografía Rosés S.A., Barcelona*

DAWN ATKINS

started her writing career in the second grade, crafting stories that included every single spelling word her teacher gave her. Since then, she's expanded her vocabulary and her publishing credits. This book is her nineteenth published book. She won the 2005 Golden Quill Award for Best Sexy Romance and has been a *Romantic Times BOOKreviews* Reviewers Choice Award finalist for Best Flipside (2005) and Best Blaze (2006). She lives in Arizona with her husband, teenage son and a butterscotch-and-white cat. Just like her heroine, her philosophy is "work hard, play hard," but she has a heck of a time making herself work at the beach. Body surfing, anyone?

To Cindi and Coco,
for inviting me into this series.

Your boundless creativity and enthusiasm made
this story a pure joy to write!

ACKNOWLEDGEMENT

Tremendous thanks to Ann Videan of Videan
Unlimited for her software marketing expertise
and moral support in the writing of this story.

Prologue

CANDY CALDER TOOK a deep breath and blurted the news that upset her as much as it would disappoint her friends. "I can't make the Malibu trip."

"What? No!" Ellie Rockwell set down Candy's order of café de Sade—the double-mocha espresso she'd created for Candy—so hard it slopped onto the polished oak bar.

"You're kidding," Sara Montgomery added in her soft Southern accent, her latte stalled mid-sip.

"I have to buckle down at work," Candy said—as much to remind herself as to explain to her friends. "My reputation is at stake."

"What's wrong with your reputation?" Ellie asked. "You work hard and you play hard. That's perfect for a software marketing genius."

"I'm hardly a genius, Ellie, but thanks."

Ellie shoved her pitch-black hair behind one ear and leaned forward, ready to fix this. Everyone who entered Dark Gothic Roast, the coffee bar that matched Ellie's glam-goth style, got a blend of java, advice and whatever help Ellie could manage.

"This was your idea," Sara said. "You said we needed

a girl-getaway." Her words made Candy grin. It hadn't been easy to convince Sara she could afford a week away from her uncle's title company where she served as his right arm, left arm and both legs.

"I know, but it can't be helped. I got a bad test result." Candy made a face.

"What kind of test?" Ellie said. "Pap smear? Mammogram? Get a second opinion before you panic, hon. They make mistakes—"

"A personality test, Ellie. SyncUp employees had to beta-test the Personality Quotient 2. I should have come out 'works hard, plays hard,' but the PQ2 says I'm 'all play, all the time.' When your brother sees that, my goose is cooked in the department." Ellie's brother Matt had just been appointed marketing vice president for SyncUp and was suddenly Candy's boss.

"Matt knows you. And when you hear my news, you'll change your mind. Listen, I got—"

"I'll still pay my share," Candy interrupted. Ellie had scored a screaming deal on a beach house through a customer who was a property manager.

"You *have* to come," Ellie pressed, "because I got—"

"You'll be fine without me, El. You'll still have Sara and the festival." The week-long event was in celebration of the second-season launch of Ellie's favorite TV show, *Sin on the Beach,* which was the only reason Ellie would agree to leave her precious coffee bar in the hands of her assistant for so long.

"This is my last chance to impress Matt before he appoints the team leaders next week." The department re-org was supposed to be hush-hush, but Candy had learned about it through Matt's secretary, who was a friend. Matt would be assigning his staff to one of five product teams and choosing a leader for each. She intended to be one of them.

"That makes the trip perfect. Matt's going to be—"

Candy grabbed Ellie's arm. "Speak of the devil. Don't look now." Over Ellie's shoulder, Candy watched Matt Rockwell stroll in, managing to look hot in boring khaki Dockers and a hopelessly wrinkled oxford shirt. His aviator glasses weren't quite retro and his chestnut hair was too shaggy to be stylish, but the overall effect was just-rolled-out-of-bed sexy and it made her tight between the thighs.

The man's rumpled kissability was partly the cause of the Thong Incident nine months ago at Matt's first happy hour at SyncUp. Because of that, the man who now held her career in his hands had an all-wrong opinion of her.

She cringed for the thousandth time.

Matt caught sight of her, reddened, paused as if he wanted to make a break for it, then soldiered on.

When he was close enough, Candy said, "Hey, Matt." Her own cheeks were idiotically on fire.

"How are you, Candy?" He nodded soberly.

"Fine. Just fine. You?"

"Fine." He cleared his throat, looked at her, breathed.

She breathed back, feeling her friends' eyes boring in.

"See you up there." Matt poked a thumb toward the ceiling, meaning the sixteenth floor, where the SyncUp office was. He looked at Ellie, then motioned down the counter, meaning he'd give his order to her assistant, so she could keep talking.

"He is *so* still into you," Ellie whispered to Candy.

"He is *so* still mortified by me. And he has a girl-friend, remember?" He'd hooked up with Jane—a coolly sophisticated attorney Ellie dubbed the Ice Princess—shortly after the Incident. He'd probably run to the woman's arms screaming "sanctuary."

"Nuh-uh. She broke up with him last week. Which brings me to my point, if you'll only let me—"

"Really?" Candy's heart did a stupid hip-hop. "I mean…so? Managers get copies of the PQ2 for sure. When Matt sees my scores, I'm dead. I have to coun-teract that."

"Do it in Malibu. That's my point. Matt will be there. He got the use-it-or-lose-it speech on his unused vacation, so I nabbed him a condo for next week, too. Just down from our beach house, as a matter of fact."

"Matt will be there? You nabbed him a…? Just down from…oh." Her heart was still doing that weird frog-jump behind her ribs. "But how will that solve my PQ2 problem?" Transfixed by the idea of Matt on vacation with her at the beach, she couldn't quite grasp Ellie's point.

"Bring work with you. Show Matt how dedicated you are." She gave Candy her patented Ellie's-on-the-case wink. "Who knows what might happen after that?"

"No way, Ellie. That ship sailed on a sea of marga-ritas." Candy wished she'd never let Ellie in on her thing for Matt. Now she simply would not let it go. The only good news was Ellie had sworn not to say a word to her brother about it.

Out of the corner of her eye, Candy saw Matt accept

his coffee—Columbian and always black. Without even trying she'd memorized stupid details about the man.

"Tell her she can't cancel, Sara," Ellie said. "Who will help me pry your fingers off your laptop and get you onto a surfboard?" Back in the day Sara had been a beach babe.

"Come on. I'm not that bad," Sara said.

Ellie and Candy spoke in unison. "Oh, yes you are." Sara groaned.

Meanwhile, Candy caught sight of Matt heading for the door. At the last second, he glanced back, straight at her, as though he'd felt her stare.

She wiggled her fingers like a moony girl, disgusted with herself. Matt nodded, a funny expression on his face. Was he picturing her in her thong? The thought made her face flame so hot she bet she could stop traffic.

She returned her attention to her friends, fighting for focus. Now where was she? Oh, yeah. "You think I can work at the beach?" A working vacation was so *not* her. And at the beach of all places. That would be downright torture.

"Work hard, play hard. That's your philosophy, right?" Ellie said. "Prove it. Do both."

Could she? She wanted to believe she could. When she'd joked in the break room about how wrong her PQ2 results were, she'd been mortified to notice that no one laughed along. They agreed with the test! And that hurt. It reminded her how her high-achieving family treated her—like a lost soul, a child whom no one took seriously. She hated that. She was determined this promotion would make her family see her through new eyes.

"You'll be away from the office, alone together. Just you and Matt and all that...*work*." Ellie waggled her brows.

Despite Ellie's ulterior motive, the idea had merit. Away from SyncUp, she and Matt could connect. Professionally, of course. She was better face-to-face anyway. And she had that proposal she'd been working up that she could show him.

She looked into her friends' hopeful faces. How could she let them down? Ellie needed me-time and Sara needed a break from indentured servitude. Someone had to make sure they got it. And what did Candy need?

Matt's respect. And maybe more confidence in her own abilities. Maybe this was just the way to get it.

"Okay," she said finally. "I'm back in."

"Whew!" Sara lifted her latte in a toast. "Here's to a week of fun, sun and men in Speedos."

"And work," Candy added. "Fun, sun, men in Speedos and *work*." The word was a sour note in the song of the moment, but at least she'd be with her friends.

"I have a good feeling about this trip," Ellie said. "I think it will change our lives."

Candy had a feeling, too. A funny, nervous one that had to do with seeing Matt in swim trunks. She made a mental note to keep her feet on the ground and her underwear covered.

1

"How did you ever talk me into this?" Candy asked Ellie as they crossed the last few yards to Matt's beach house. "Mixing work and play is like chasing a tequila shot with a piña colada—guaranteed puke-fest."

"Trust me," Ellie said. "It'll be fine."

"And this thing weighs a ton." She shifted the antique laptop she'd borrowed from the SyncUp IT department to her other shoulder and wiggled her toes in her sandals to relieve the irritation of grinding sand. The beach was meant for bare feet, not shoes, for God's sake.

"You should have swiped Sara's computer so she'd have no excuse not to be in a bikini this minute," Ellie said.

"I can't believe she sneaked that little printer into her bag."

"Fighting your nature is not easy," Ellie said.

"No kidding." That was as clear to Candy as the Malibu sky overhead, where no cloud troubled the bright blue expanse. Her whole body ached to toss this computer onto the nearest porch, grab a tiki drink and frolic in the foam.

"This will work," Ellie said again, squeezing Candy's upper arm. "I know it will."

Candy blinked against the sunlight glancing off the sparkling water. It was all so tempting—the gently swooshing waves, the kids shrieking as they dashed into the water, the spectacular hunks jogging by—tan and muscular and ready to play.

But this was no time for Candy's inner girl-gone-wild to lift her pale face to the sun. She had a mission, dammit, and her future at SyncUp hung in the balance.

On the other hand, she'd worn her yellow bikini beneath the white capris and white blouse she'd knotted at her waist, and her straw beach bag held a towel, sunscreen and flip-flops—just in case she squeezed in some beach time. She was prepared to seize whatever pleasure she could out of this trip.

She fished her cell phone out of the tight pocket of her capris to be sure it was on loud ring. Sara was due to fake a work call after they reached Matt's place.

A big dog wearing a red bandanna galloped up and snuffled Candy's hand, then back-stepped away, inviting her to toss something—her phone?

"Wish I could, Bucko," she said, "but I need it."

With a little yelp, the dog galloped off in search of someone who understood what the beach was for. Candy sighed. Maybe later she'd catch up with the cheerful guy. For now, she stood at the bottom of Matt's stairs.

"Ready to dazzle my brother with your work ethic?" Ellie asked.

Candy rubbed the top of her nose. "Yep. All raw from the grindstone."

"Showtime, then." Ellie started upward.

Candy grabbed her arm. "No ad-libbing, now. No hints, no winks, no nudges. Matt and I will never be a notch on your matchmaker's belt."

"Whatever you say." Ellie's cheerful concession was too easy, Candy knew, vowing to watch her friend closely.

Ellie bounded up the stairs and Candy followed, her heart pounding as loudly in her ears as Ellie's knock.

When Matt opened the door, Candy's heart took a header into her stomach. The way it had before that mortifying kiss gone wrong, when she'd landed on her back—legs in the air, tiger thong on display, dignity out the window.

"Hello," Matt said to Ellie, then caught sight of her. "And Candy?" His eyes grabbed her, a piercing blue, even through his glasses. When Matt looked at her, he really *looked*. As though she were a tangled computer code he must decipher or die.

Read me, baby, she wanted to say. *Read me all night long.*

His intense focus appealed to her. Also, his calm restraint, beneath which he was probably hotter than hot. Like the mild-mannered alter ego of the all-powerful man of steel.

Steel…hmm. The thought of his steeliest part made her insides melt like a frozen daiquiri in the sun.

Stop that. Work, not play.

"In the flesh," she said. *Flesh? Did you have to say flesh?* She rushed on. "When Ellie told me you'd be here, I was relieved *someone* would understand how to work on vacation." She patted the laptop. Something tinkled and dropped inside the bag. Nothing vital, she hoped.

"*You're* working? On vacation?" The emphasis on *you're* wounded her, but Matt blinked. He didn't seem to have intended to insult her. She knew him to be a straightforward guy who stuck to the facts. He wasn't into the nuances of diplomacy.

"I practically had to drag her here," Ellie said. "She wanted to cancel because of her project."

"What project?" He gave Candy another shot of his blue zingers.

"I'm working on something for Ledger Lite." The accounting software was one of SyncUp's bread-and-butter products. Version 2.0 was set for beta testing and she'd had a great idea she hoped would impress him. "Would you consider taking a look at what I've got?"

His eyes dipped to her breasts, then up, as if she'd invited him to peek at her attributes. Heat rushed through her, but she rattled breathlessly onward. "I wouldn't bother you, but it's crucial before the beta launches, so I thought why not?"

Clunk. Woof!

She turned to see that the beach dog had dropped a red Frisbee at her feet and now quivered with excitement, expecting her to throw it.

"Your dog?" Matt asked with a wry half-smile.

"No, but we've met." The dog recognized her as a kindred spirit, no doubt. She bent for the Frisbee, but "Flight of the Bumblebee" played from her pocket, so she held up a finger to signify business before pleasure and dug for her cell.

The dog moaned in an agony of disappointment.

Her pocket was so tight that when she got the phone out, it slipped to the porch. The retriever grabbed it and bounded away.

Crap. Candy set the computer on the porch, kicked off her sandals and dashed after the dog. Matt had already headed off. So much for her professional impression.

Seconds later, they were playing keep-away with the nimble canine, feinting and lunging and missing, until Candy finally jumped onto its furry middle and held the dog still so Matt could pry the phone from its jaws.

After Candy let him go, the dog jumped up and down, eager for another toss of the expensive chew toy.

Matt helped Candy up. The warmth of his hand zinged through her, the way it had when he'd boosted her to her feet after the thong flash. He wiped the phone with the bottom of his oxford shirt, giving her a drool-worthy glimpse of a muscular belly. Hmm. Earnest, gallant *and* buff.

He handed her the cleaned-up phone. "Great tackle."

"Great teamwork," she said, pressing home her point about her work skills.

The dog whined piteously for attention.

"Easy, boy." Matt patted him, then crouched to read the tag dangling from the middle of the dog's bandanna. "Looks like your name is Radar, huh?" He scrubbed the top of the dog's head with his knuckles.

Candy lowered herself to pet the dog, too, meeting Matt's eyes over its back. She felt trapped in his gaze even after Radar lost interest in them and galloped off.

Matt leaned closer, fingers outstretched. She had the

crazy thought that he wanted to kiss her again, which couldn't be true. But electricity blew through her all the same, making her feel swoony and weak.

Mid-reach, Matt's fingers stilled. "You have some, uh, sand." He brushed his own cheek to show her where.

"Oh. Right." She smoothed away the grains. That night, she'd mistaken Matt's swipe at a dab of prickly-pear margarita for a smooch attempt. No wonder she'd gotten confused, what with all the heat crackling between them. Except maybe that had been the big black speaker on the stand beside them, which Matt dislodged when Candy moved in to make the kiss easier.

He caught the speaker, but missed Candy, who toppled off her platform sandals into thong-baring infamy.

"You got it," Matt said now, smiling. She imagined tugging off his glasses, then stripping to the skin to go at it like sex-starved beach trash.

Bad, bad Candy. She sighed, smiled and stood to call Sara back, praying dog drool hadn't gummed her phone's works.

Sara answered immediately. "What happened?"

"My phone got away from me," she said, shooting a smile at Matt. "Sorry."

"Okay, so… I'm your colleague calling with the stats you needed. Seventy-five percent, three point two, two to one ratio…blah, blah, et cetera, et cetera."

With Matt staring at her it was tough to fake a business tone, but Candy did her best. "Thanks much. I'll grab that e-mail ASAP. Great." She clicked off and slid the phone into her pocket. "Some numbers I need.

Can I download e-mail inside your place? Maybe show you my ideas while I'm at it?"

"I guess. Sure." He looked baffled by the suggestion, but he headed toward the porch, where Ellie beamed down at them. *You look so cute together.*

"We're going to work now," Candy said, telling Ellie with her eyes it was time to scoot.

"Sure. I'll just check Matt's supplies and then you can get to it."

"My sister, the mother hen," Matt said, sounding affectionately exasperated. He winked at Candy and it went right through her like sexy lightning. Oh, she was weak.

"I have food," he called to Ellie, following her inside, where she flung open cupboards and yanked open the fridge, clucking like the hen Matt had compared her to.

"HoHos, Cheetos, Dr. Pepper and beer? You call that food?"

"Sounds good to me," Candy said with a shrug. More than once she and Matt had vied for the last sack of Cheetos or package of HoHos in the SyncUp snack machines. They shared junk food preferences if nothing else.

"Did you remember sunscreen?" Ellie asked, hands on hips. When Matt shrugged, she sighed. "I'll pick up some. Along with some healthy food."

"I can feed myself, Ellie." He paused. "There's no point arguing, is there?"

"Not really, no."

"Do what you must then." He sighed, but he was smiling. Obviously, Matt had plenty of experience with his sister's nurturing ways. Candy liked the rapport between them.

Setting her ancient laptop beside Matt's razor-thin model already open to e-mail, Candy noticed the neat spread of folders beside it, proving that Matt was a master at working vacations. He was already at it and they'd all barely arrived.

"But what about entertaining yourself?" Ellie said. "You're not going to sit here all week at the computer. You work too hard. Both of you. Especially you, Candy."

Liar, liar, pants on fire. But Candy loved Ellie for overacting on her behalf.

Ellie snatched a flyer from behind a magnet on the refrigerator and carried it to where Candy and Matt stood at the table. "Look at all these *Sin on the Beach* festival events." She handed Matt the flyer and lowered her voice. "No moping now. There are other fish in the sea." She was obviously referring to the breakup with Ice Princess Jane.

"I'll be fine, Ellie," Matt said. "Don't worry about me."

"Then I guess my work here is done." Ellie gave a pointed look at Candy, then hip-swayed to the door. Because Matt had moved to the kitchen, Candy was able to shoot her a quick thumbs-up as she left.

"Can I get you something to drink?" he called from the open refrigerator. "A beer?"

"Water is fine, since I'm working and all." Was that overkill? Maybe. She sighed.

She couldn't help thinking how great it would be to just kick back in this cozy bungalow with a beer and Matt and those blue-sky eyes of his. But that was the old Candy. The new one had a vital task to achieve.

She shifted her laptop and it knocked one of Matt's files to the floor, fanning paper across the white tiles.

The first doc she retrieved was a PQ2 report with Matt's name on a label at the top. Also attached to it was a pink Post-It note in the bold script of their CEO, Scott Bayer. *See me re: changes!*

Matt arrived with her glass of water and his beer.

She handed him the report form. "You took the PQ2?"

"Scott required all the managers to take it."

"What changes is he talking about? In the test?"

Matt gave a humorless laugh. "No. In the managers. He wants us to address the weaknesses the test revealed."

"What weaknesses could you possibly have?" she teased.

"Exactly." He grinned his great half smile. "According to the PQ2, I'm low on sociability." He sat next to her. "Do I strike you as antisocial, Candy?" He looked at her so directly her heart tightened in her chest. "Be honest."

"You don't chit-chat. You're pretty direct. I'd say you're more nonsocial than actually *anti*social."

"Nonsocial. Yeah. I like that. I guess I don't get the function of small talk. Make your point and move on. Why waste time?"

"But informal talk eases tension, makes people feel comfortable—safe to take risks. A little back-and-forth about the weekend, the Suns game or the nephew's bar mitzvah greases the wheel of ideas, gets people psyched to tackle tough issues."

He paused, pondering her words, she could tell. She'd never dug up a rationale for what seemed so obvious to her.

"I suppose that makes sense," Matt mused. "The proximate issue is that Scott expects me to score some clients at the convention. It's next month, so I've got to get better at backslapping and schmoozing right away."

"Sounds like fun."

He smiled. "To you, sure." He gave her that look that made her wiring crackle. "But I'm not you."

No, wait. The crackling was coming from her borrowed laptop, which was grinding to life with agonizing slowness and enough noise that Candy expected some of Ellie's espresso to drip out.

"For what it's worth, the PQ2 got me wrong, too," Candy said.

"How so?"

"It made me seem like I don't take work seriously."

"You? No! How could that be?" His eyes twinkled at her. "Maybe because of the time you brought in all those cans of Silly String and made a mess in the lab?"

"Everyone was getting cranky. We needed a break. And it cleaned up easy."

"Or how about when you spiked the Halloween punch?"

"Come on. It was a party. I warned Valerie first."

"She was pregnant, right?" He nodded. "Your costume was…interesting."

She'd dressed as a zombie hooker, which would have been fine, except she'd only convinced a few people to dress up, so she sort of stood out.

"Happy workers are productive workers, Matt. There are studies that show the benefits of morale building and—"

"As I recall, three people went home too drunk to work, someone tossed their pumpkin cookies into a trash can and everyone else but Val slept away the afternoon over their keyboards."

He was smiling, but light glanced off his lenses and she couldn't tell if he was amused or making fun of her. The Halloween party had been early in Matt's time at SyncUp. If she'd known that six months later he'd be her boss, she might have been more careful about how she behaved around him.

"As *I* recall, you laughed a lot. Plus, you won the one-on-one wastepaper basketball tournament the next month."

"Your idea, too, correct?"

"We'd put in two sixty-hour weeks on the Payroll Plus revision. We needed a break." She'd come up with the idea of a modified basketball game using office chairs with trash cans on file cabinets for baskets and wadded printouts as the balls.

"That was fun," he mused.

"And afterward, we were refreshed for more work. Work hard, play hard, that's my philosophy." She hoped he'd buy that. It sounded like a bluff. That's how her family would see it, considering her history. She'd been erratic in college, uncertain in the work world and switched jobs a lot. Her parents, on the other hand, had built a business from scratch and her brothers had beelined from law school to successful law practices without an eye-blink of doubt. The four of them thought her a flake and the idea seared her with hot shame.

"I see." Matt seemed to be fighting a grin.

"The point is the PQ2 got me wrong." She spoke too fiercely. "It mischaracterized you, too, remember?"

He didn't respond and she was afraid she'd sounded too defensive.

"Anyway, I want to show you what I'm thinking on Ledger Lite." She put her finger on the touch pad, except at that instant the machine ominously ceased grinding. The screen was white—half built.

"Damn!" She banged the side of the laptop. "The tech guys said this unit was a workhorse."

"Let me take a look." Matt turned the computer toward him, swamping her with the scent of lime and warm man. He clicked keys, then rebooted with three nimble-looking, knowing-seeming fingers.

She couldn't help imagining what they might do to her private touch pad. She shifted away from him, bumping the computer cord. There was a crackle and the screen went dead black.

"Ah. Maybe a short in the transformer," Matt said. He unplugged the cord assembly and carried it to the kitchen.

Now what? She hadn't printed out anything since the spreadsheets were huge and the artwork mock-up looked better on screen. If her computer was dead, so was her plan.

It wasn't as though he could actually fix the damn cord, but Matt needed to escape Candy Calder. She smelled as sweet as her name and inhaling near her made it impossible to hold a thought that didn't have sex in it.

He pawed through the drawers looking for a Phillips screwdriver, but had to settle for a paring knife, which he twisted into the tiny bolts on the transformer box.

This predicament had Ellie's fingerprints all over it. She must have figured that Candy would cheer him up after Jane.

The odd thing was that the breakup hadn't been as hard on him as he'd expected. Maybe he was numb or still in shock, but he'd felt mostly relief, which didn't seem like the proper response to the end of a nine-month relationship.

Either way, he had no business hanging with Candy Calder and her mischievous eyes the same violet as the SyncUp logo. Or those puffy lips of hers. He'd watched her wrap them around a margarita glass that night after his first week at SyncUp and wanted—no, craved—a taste. Then he'd fumbled the kiss and knocked her on her ass.

The woman threw him, made him act herky-jerky and stupid. And now she'd dragged an old computer here to show him her *work?* What was her angle? It couldn't be the same as Ellie's. No way would Candy allow Ellie to plot a hookup. After that goofed kiss, Candy thought him an oaf. Probably had had a good laugh with her SyncUp friends. And everyone at SyncUp loved Candy. The whole place rang with her laughter.

The husky honey of her voice warmed him straight through, made it hard to think about anything but her.

The PQ2 had nailed her and her playfulness, all right. It had nailed him, too, for that matter. He was non-social, as she'd said. He valued alone time, hated mindless chatter and worked hard. Maybe too hard, but he loved what he did, dammit, and what was wrong with spending time with what he loved?

Something was. Even Jane had gotten on his case.

Supposedly that's why she'd broken up with him. What had she called him? *A workaholic with no capacity for relaxation.* Then she'd gotten nasty. *You wouldn't know fun if it threw you a surprise party.*

That was a case of the pot calling the kettle black, if he'd ever heard one. A commitment to their careers was something they shared. Hell, Jane routinely put in sixty-hour weeks at her law firm. He had no problem with that. They'd fit their relationship around their schedules just fine.

Fun had its place, but hard work and dedication were what had earned him the VP spot at a hot software firm. And now, to keep it, he'd have to learn to…chitchat. God.

He was an engineer first, a marketer second and nowhere in there an ass-kissing backslapper.

Ironic that he'd been discussing his problem with Candy, who was the most social person he knew.

The last screw emerged from the transformer box, so he tried separating the two halves. No use. There seemed to be an adhesive. He was prying it open with the knife blade when Candy approached.

"You getting it off?" she asked softly, inches away.

Her closeness and her words made him stab himself in the thumb. "Damn." Blood oozed, so he pressed his index finger against the spot.

"You cut yourself?" Candy yanked his wrist up into the air.

"What are you doing?" he asked as calmly as he could with her breasts right…*there,* sticking out at him. So *alert.*

"Elevating the injury above your heart, of course."

She was so short she had to tilt her head up to talk to him. Her big eyes invited him to dive in and drown.

"It's fine," he said.

"Are you sure?"

"I'm sure."

She lowered his arm and leaned in to study the little nick, her perfumed hair tickling his chin, her fingers warm on his skin.

"Not even bleeding, see," he said, backing away from the same heat he'd felt on Oaf Night. "Your computer's dead, Candy."

"How can I show you my work then?" She seemed truly upset. What was her game? "I know! Can I borrow your computer? Pick up what I've got on e-mail and get someone at the office to grab my desktop files?" She was moving closer to him again, digging in, making him dizzy. He wished to God it was loss of blood making it so hard to think, not the Candy Effect.

"Except then how can you work?" she said, frowning. "If I take your laptop?"

"I'll be fine," he said, fighting for balance. "This is supposed to be my vacation. I should probably get out more, be more social…or whatever." What the hell was he saying?

She studied him, her head tilted, figuring something out. He could practically hear the gears whirring. "I can help you, you know," she said slowly, her honeyed voice melting his insides. "We can help each other."

"We can?" How did her lips stay so red without lipstick? He remembered her muscular legs waving in the air that night. And she'd worn striped panties that disappeared completely between the cheeks of her—

"You loan me your computer and let me show you my ideas and I'll teach you how to schmooze. How's that?"

"I loan you my...? You show me...? I don't see how...really...that's possible." He had no business spending time with a woman who could say the word *schmooze* and make him forget his own name.

"Come on. It'll be fun, Matt."

Matt. Yeah, that was his name. Now he remembered. He shook his head, attempting to clear it.

Woof!

Through the screen door, Matt saw the golden retriever they'd wrestled for Candy's cell phone.

"Radar votes yes," Candy said.

"Then how can I say no?" He was taking his cues from a dog now? Looking into Candy's violet eyes, he had the feeling this wasn't the last crazy thing he would do this week.

Not even close.

2

THIS COULD WORK, Candy thought, except for the fact that it meant spending more time with Matt than she'd intended. She'd have to keep her libido under control— say padlocked in a deep freeze at the bottom of the ocean?

Her sexual response to him got stronger with each moment they spent together. It was like standing in a candy store when you were on a diet—just plain torture.

She'd never been that big on sexual denial, either, and it would be tough enough to test her work-hard-play-hard philosophy as it was.

She was only human.

On the other hand, this plan was a chance to prove her worth to SyncUp and to correct Matt's bad impression of her at the same time. He clearly had one, judging from his attitude about her Halloween party stunts. No doubt he'd heard about Jared, too.

After the Thong Incident, she'd concluded she had a thing for analytical types and gone out with a SyncUp engineer. Jared was cute and smart and funny, but there'd been no sparks. She'd kissed him good-night to be nice and the grateful bozo turned it into *The Story of O* around the company.

Rumor had it they'd done it on the roof. Yes, they'd been up there, but only to look at the altimeter Jared had built as part of a science education package he was coding.

With a reputation at SyncUp as a sex fiend, Candy had to nix any hints of that around Matt.

Radar whined for her to come play. He was as annoying as her sex drive around Matt. She could not be tempted by either one. Business first, pleasure second. And only if there was time.

She moved to Matt's computer, ready to log in and gather what she could by e-mail. She would contact Freeda, the department's secretary, about retrieving her desktop files.

Matt joined her at the table, standing over her. "So, uh, how do you see the other part working?"

She looked up from the keyboard. "What other part?"

"The social stuff? What do you propose?"

"You want to start there?" She could see he was concerned. "All right. Let's make a plan."

"A plan?"

"To turn you into Mr. Networking. Backslap Boy. Fun Guy. Whatever you want to call the new, more social you." She grabbed her notepad and headed for the sofa, pausing to pick up the magenta festival flyer. "Let's look at what's here we can work with, huh?" She motioned him into the living room and dropped onto the blue canvas sofa.

He sat close enough to swamp her with lime and spice.

"So what interests you?" she asked, making a bullet point on the paper.

When he didn't answer right away, she looked at him and found him staring at her mouth. "Uh…what?

What interests me?" He cleared his throat, then shifted on the sofa.

"Yes. What do you do for fun?"

He rubbed the back of his neck. "I don't know. I read. E-mail loops. Blogs. Internet stuff. Some programming I'm working on for fun. I shoot some hoops."

He'd thrown in the basketball to sound like a regular guy, she'd bet, instead of a work-obsessed nerd. He wasn't a nerd. He was too handsome, too aware of other people. He was just serious, quiet and private. Locked in his own head. She found that strangely soothing. Maybe as a contrast with her own restless energy. It might be nice to share solitude with someone. Until she got bored. It would be like meditation. She'd tried it, but could only bear a few seconds of letting her thoughts float away before she had to go after them with a butterfly net and a notepad.

"In short, you work," she said. "What you read are trade journals and e-zines, right? Your Internet loops and blogs are with marketing and software groups. Am I right?"

He shrugged. "Focus got me where I am, Candy. That's what Scott's forgetting with this whole changes-must-be-made bit. That's my strength and I won't undermine that."

"We'll just tweak your style a bit." She made a twisting gesture. "You'll barely feel a pinch."

When he grinned, she realized it was a triumph to earn a smile from such a serious guy. This close, she noticed a sexy chip in one of his incisors—a hint there was a bad boy in there somewhere. She'd love to talk him out to play.

Another time. On another planet. In an alternate universe.

"I know what I'm doing," she said, hoping she did. "Before you were a driven software engineer and marketing strategist, where did you get your kicks?"

He stared up at the ceiling. "Let's see. In high school I was in a band—but what high school kid wasn't?"

"What instrument?"

"Bass guitar."

"How cool. I always had a thing for sexy bass players. Silent…moody…deep."

He shook his head. "Did you ever consider we might be silent because we had nothing to say?"

"Don't destroy my fantasy." She covered her ears with her hands, pleased when he chuckled. "What kind of music did you play?"

"Ska, rhythm & blues. Top 40 hits for parties. We weren't together that long."

"Long enough to get laid, though?"

"There was that." He winced with pretend guilt. She could see him with a guitar at his hips, moving to the music, flashing that chipped tooth at the girls who caught his eye. Desire shivered through her.

To hide her reaction, she held out the flyer so they could both see it. "Doesn't look like they've got a battle of the bands going, so what other hobbies have you got?"

"Photography. I took a couple of classes."

"Photography? Oh. Hang on… Yes! Here. The Hot Shot Photo Scavenger Hunt tomorrow night. It's sponsored by a cell-phone company. Does your cell take pictures?"

"Sure." He leaned toward her to dig into his back pocket for his phone, and for that fleeting moment, she was hyperaware of his body, his muscles, how he smelled, how easy it would be to lie back on the couch and take him with her.

Finally, he sat back, ending the sensory assault, flipped open the phone and handed it to her.

"This is the same model I have," she said, managing to sound normal. She clicked into the photos he'd stored, curious about what he'd saved. "You saved pictures of *computers?*"

"I was checking out monitors," he said.

She kept clicking and found shots of digital cameras...shelves in a computer store...sales displays. "Where are your friends? Your mom? Ellie, for God's sake?"

"I have pictures of them. Just not on my phone." He reached for the phone, but she held it away.

"I'm not finished looking." He kept reaching while she playfully held back. His arm brushed her breasts, giving her a tingling rush.

He pulled away immediately. "Sorry."

"Not your fault." Matt had taken the blame for the Thong Incident, too, which had clearly been a two-person catastrophe.

She focused on the phone photos, fighting the waves she still felt. Then she hit the jackpot—a shot of Matt wearing Mickey Mouse ears. His dark hair curled messily from beneath the brim and he managed to look grave and sweet at the same time.

"This is so cute," she said, showing it to him.

"God. Ellie," Matt said. "One of her customers had just been to Disneyland. You know how Ellie gets."

"I'm glad she took this. It's proof you *can* loosen up."

"So you think I'm uptight?" He seemed amused by the idea.

"Not uptight. Just restrained. Controlled." Everything she wasn't, but needed to learn how to be. Or at least how to appear to be when it counted.

Part of her rebelled at that. *Take me as I am, dammit. Can't you see I can be silly* and *brilliant?*

But she knew that wasn't easy to accept. She remembered when she'd told her family she'd left the ad agency to work for SyncUp. They looked at each other the same way. *Not again.*

They'd been polite and encouraging, but there was no mistaking their weariness. *When will she grow up, figure it out, settle down?*

They just didn't get her. She had a plan and this promotion was key. She was building contacts, networking, getting experience. In five years or so, she would open up her own agency, maybe with a partner.

"You okay?" Matt had noticed her preoccupation.

"Sure. I'm fine." She smiled, sorry she'd gotten distracted.

"So, you think all I have to do is slap Mickey Mouse ears on my head and people will buy SyncUp products from me?"

"Whatever works, Matt," she said, smiling. "Actually, though, now that we're talking about it, a camera is a great networking tool. Bring a camera to an event and everyone's your friend. You have a good digital, I assume?"

"Not with me. I bought the new Canon EOS 350D, eight megapixel, an upgrade from the 300D. It's got—"

"Forget the specs, Matt. Will it fit in your pocket?"

"I have a case for it."

"The idea is to keep it with you at all times. When you're at the convention, take photos and you have an excuse to exchange business cards so you can e-mail the snaps. Instant leads."

He gazed at her, a smile tracing his lips. "You're good."

The words would have been a sexual come-on from any other guy. From Matt they were straight praise. She was chagrined to notice they aroused her anyway. She was tuned into him, hyperaware, probably from the long-ago crush, which seemed to be getting worse.

She stayed on task. "So, tomorrow night we'll do this photo hunt."

"What are we supposed to take pictures of?" He tugged the flyer closer. "Exactly what are 'hot shots'?"

There were no specifics listed. "Sexy stuff, I'd guess. It's the *Sin on the Beach* festival. Remember? Sights you'd see in a *Girls Gone Wild* commercial or, say, spring break in Florida. Anything goes."

He seemed to chew that over, work it out like an equation to be solved for X. "So I'm supposed to talk women into taking off their clothes for me?"

"You'll have no trouble."

"Are you kidding?"

"Not at all. You're a hot guy." She shrugged.

"You think I'm hot?" He honed in on her.

"Absolutely."

He shook his head, as if he thought she was being polite.

"I'm serious. You're built. You're good-looking." She surveyed him. Sunlight flashed off his glasses. "You should ditch these, though." She tugged them from his face, being playful, but was startled at how close his electric-blue eyes suddenly were. The moment was abruptly intimate, like being naked with someone for the first time, and she could hardly breathe.

"You have great eyes," she said, lowering his glasses to her lap to hide the fact her fingers had started to shake.

"How am I supposed to see?"

"Get contacts."

"Too much hassle. Little plastic floppy things." He rubbed his fingers together, then shook them, as if to rid himself of the clingy objects. "I don't know how you stand them."

"How did you know I wear them?"

"They swim over your irises."

"Oh. Well, then." He'd watched her closely enough to catch that detail? Awareness tingled through her. "They're a lot easier to use these days. You can wear them for a month, even at night. You really should try them."

He just looked at her.

"Will you do it? Try contacts?"

"Maybe." But he wouldn't without a nudge, she could tell. Men just didn't jump on stuff like that.

"Why don't we get you some while we're here? They'll enhance your sociability."

"You think?" His eyebrows dipped and his forehead crinkled, considering the idea.

"Sure. Glasses are barriers, creating distance between you and the other person. Without them you seem closer, warmer, more available."

"Is that how you see me now? Closer? More available?"

Oh, yeah. She managed a simple nod. If he hadn't made the question sound like a scientific inquiry, she would have attacked him right here on the couch.

They were alone, breathing in synch, inches apart, with Matt looking at her in the serious, steady way that always got to her. Attraction swelled like the waves surging onto the beach a few yards beyond his door.

She crossed her thighs against the ache she felt and strove for good sense. "While we're at it, we should do something about your look."

"My look?"

"You're a hot software designer, Matt. You need an edge. A haircut, for one thing. And definitely new clothes."

"What's wrong with my clothes?" He looked down at his blue oxford shirt and khaki shorts. "They're clean. They match."

"For one thing, this is not beachwear." She let her eyes travel down his body. "You need a tank top." She eyed his arms, envisioning bared shoulders, fanned deltoids. "A Hawaiian shirt, maybe—" she kept looking down "—and some board shorts." She realized she was staring at his zipper, so she jerked up her eyes and met his curious gaze.

Embarrassed, she babbled on. "New business clothes, too. What you wear is too traditional. We can do it at the mall here. It'll be kind of a makeover."

"A makeover? You mean one of those *Queer Eye-Straight Guy* deals? No way am I shoving up my sleeves or layering." He held up his hands in a stop gesture.

"Nothing major. We'll just give you some verve."

"*Verve?* That's way too gay."

"Forget verve, then. Think of it as a software update. Matt, version 2.0."

"I don't know…"

"Sure you do. A new image is half the battle with Scott. We update your look, teach you to network and—poof—you're the fabulous marketing VP Scott wants."

"That's pretty superficial, don't you think?"

"Everything's perception, Matt. We both know that. Shaping opinions, creating an image is part of our craft."

"So, we're marketing me to Scott?"

"Exactly."

"You make it sound easy."

"It is. You said it yourself. I'm good." *Which is why you want me as a team leader.* Hell, before the trip was over, he might just offer her the job. "So, are you with me?"

"I guess so." He hesitated, then tried to smile. "You seem to know what you're doing."

"I promise you won't be sorry," she said softly, vowing to do her very best for him, to help him without pushing him too far out of his comfort range.

She slid his glasses back in place, grateful for the barrier between them, aware they were both holding their breath. She noticed the beauty mark high on his right cheek, the crinkles that fanned out from both eyes, hinting at the humor behind his seriousness.

"I'll pull up the mall's Web site and see about morning appointments. Sound good?"

"I guess I'm just grateful you're not suggesting I get my teeth bonded."

"You mean fix that chip? Oh, never. That's proof you've got some bad boy in you."

"Oh, I'm bad, all right. I write code without off-site backup and drink milk straight from the carton."

She laughed. "I didn't realize how funny you are."

"You bring it out in me." He hesitated, as if he'd said more than he'd intended. "In everyone, I mean."

"Thanks," she said, warmed by his words, by this admission that she'd affected him in a good way. Again she was imbued with the determination to help him, to do this right, to prove herself in this new way.

"So, back to the festival," she said, staring down at the flyer, shy about her surge of pride. Aware, also, of Matt's close gaze, the way he studied her. It was unnerving and reassuring at the same time.

"So, what else can we do? You say you played basketball, so let's see what sports are going on. Ah, here we go. Beach volleyball. Starting in—" she looked at her watch "—half an hour. Let's do that. We'll meet some people, which will be good practice for you. After that, we can come back here and I'll show you my stuff."

"Beg your pardon?" His eyes dropped to her bikini, which peeked from the sides of her blouse.

"My *marketing* stuff, Matt."

He turned bright red. "Sorry."

"It's okay. You're human." She pushed at his arm in a friendly way, but her fingers stayed a moment too long. Having such a polite guy unable to keep from staring at her chest was dead sexy.

"I'm not usually so rude. Around you…I don't know. You're so…*lively.*"

"Lively?" Was that code for her being blatantly sexual? A party girl, in other words? That thought was a cold stab. "I'm more than you think I am," she said lightly, not wanting to reveal her hurt. She usually didn't take such quick offense, but the whole PQ2 thing and the promotion pressure had thrown off her confidence.

"That's true of most of us, isn't it?"

"Sure. I guess." Everyone got pigeonholed to some degree, but not everyone got padlocked in as she'd been by her family. And not everyone could lose credibility at work over their reputation, either. She'd had enough of false impressions and she needed her time with Matt to fix this for good.

"Do you want to change?" Matt asked.

"What's wrong with how I am?" Had he seen her PQ2 already?

"I mean for the volleyball game?" He nodded at her outfit.

"Oh. Change *my clothes.* Sorry." She laughed, feeling foolish. *Lighten up.* "We haven't got time really. I'll just get more comfortable." She took off her blouse, since it would constrict her arms, then crouched into a block to test her pants. "Too tight," she concluded and undid the zipper to step out of her capris.

Afterward, Matt seemed to have to drag his gaze up to her face. She'd just changed in front of him, after all.

"Better?" he asked, swallowing over what must have been a dry throat.

"Sure," she said, flattered that he seemed to have to struggle to stop staring at her. The bottom of her bikini wasn't cut particularly high and the top barely showed the curve of her breasts, but Matt seemed utterly stunned.

"You'll want to lose the shirt," she said, nodding at him.

He took it off and tossed it to the couch.

Now it was her turn to stare. Definitely buff, with an attractive line of dark hair that began low on his chest and pointed toward glory.

"Candy? You okay?"

"Yeah. Just checking." She pretended to consider his biceps. "You've got a faint tan line, but your olive skin means you'll only need a kiss of sun."

"You're worried about my tan?"

"A spray-on touch-up wouldn't hurt."

"What?"

She grinned. "Kidding! Nothing extreme. Maybe just a chemical peel? Kidding," she added before he could object.

"I have the feeling I'm going to regret this," he said, but his eyes twinkled. "I look okay for the game?" He stood back so she could check him out.

Naked to the waist, he was awe-inspiring. Even wearing boring khaki shorts. "Lose the belt," was all she said.

He whipped the leather smoothly from the loops, his eyes on her the entire time, and her body went electric. *Don't stop,* she wanted to say. *Take it all off.*

"Shoes, too," she breathed, kicking off her own sandals.

He did likewise and there they stood, inches apart, with next to no clothes between them. Her bikini seemed like tiny paper-thin triangles and Matt's shorts a mere patch of khaki. They were so close to naked heaven.

Was he aroused? She dared a glance at his zipper, where she thought she detected a bulge. Oh. Her own sex ached madly.

This was wrong. She forced herself to move, bending to grab her clothes, then Matt's shirt. She shoved them all, plus their shoes, into her straw bag.

"I'll get my, uh, sunglasses," Matt said, bolting away from her toward the hall. Thank God.

Candy hightailed it outside, where she felt better. She dug her toes into the warm sand, inhaled the salt smell, took in that white glow the air at the beach always had. Seagulls cried and spun overhead. Down the shore, children shrieked happily.

The breeze lifted her hair and she tilted her face to the sun for a moment of pleasure. She had work to do, of course, and an attraction to ignore, but she was at the *beach* and it was glorious.

She turned to find Matt watching her from his porch. Even in the old-school sunglasses, he looked hot. With a good cut, contacts and well-tailored clothes, women would fall all over themselves to get to him.

As he headed toward her, she wondered who would be next. Someone big on career like Ice Princess Jane, no doubt. Someone chic and cool, Blackberry at her fingertips, pricey merlots in her temp-controlled wine closet. Thinking of Ms. Next-in-Line cooled Candy's hots for Matt, which was a very good thing.

When he reached her, she fished out sunscreen, put some on her hands and held out the tube to him.

While she applied the cream to her arms, he rubbed some briskly between his broad palms, then smeared it over his face and shoulders, leaving white streaks everywhere.

"You have to rub it in," she said and smoothed the liquid into his nose and across his cheekbones, blocking her awareness of how close she was and how nice his skin felt.

"Turn around," she said, thinking that would help. She was a glutton for punishment, she realized, surveying the muscular expanse of his back. With a sigh, she started in on the firm surface of Matt's shoulders and upper back, enjoying the slide of his muscles, lingering longer than strictly necessary, her mind sluggish with pleasure.

Why can't we sleep together again?

He's your boss. You want him to promote you.

Oh, yeah. That. She was showing him how smart and balanced and hard-working she was. How dedicated and responsible. How—

"You about done there?" he asked, turning.

"Uh, sure. Just being thorough."

"Shall I do you?" he asked, low and slow.

Not that he meant anything by the suggestive words, but they gave her *thoughts*. "That'd be great." She handed him the tube, turning her back.

His fingers pressed into her skin as he rubbed slowly and carefully, even under her shoulder straps. He was so very *thorough*. As he kept working, she couldn't help but think that one little tug and her top would drop and he'd have more to rub than he'd bargained for. Her knees turned to water.

"You okay?" he asked.

"I think you got it," she said, turning to grab the tube from his hand.

He looked startled, still holding his hand out.

"We'll be late," she said, hurrying toward the water, hoping it would be chilly enough to shock her out of her sensual lethargy.

Matt caught up and they walked the edge of the surf, letting the waves brush their toes, then retreat in foamy whispers.

The water was full of swimmers and bodysurfers. Young boys on Boogie boards tumbled like acrobats into the surf, heedless of pain or danger.

The shore was crowded with sunbathers under colorful umbrellas, lying on towels, surrounded by ice chests and beach toys, tossing balls or Frisbees.

"I love the beach," she said, determined to enjoy every moment of it she could.

"Me, too," Matt said. "I'm glad Ellie got me out here."

"She said you had to use up vacation time."

"I did. I tend to get too focused."

"It's easy when you love your work," she said, but she'd never had extra vacation to use up. She'd had to take a two-day advance to make a Tahoe trip with friends to a ski lodge.

"Actually, Candy, I'm glad you came over. I might have parked myself in front of my laptop and missed all this." He gestured out at the sparkling line between sky and sea.

"I'm glad I could be what you need," Candy said,

the words far too intimate. Her traitorous heart fluttered in her chest.

You're what I need, too.

For my career, she reminded herself firmly. They were helping each other. This was all about SyncUp and their working relationship. The nearly naked volleyball game, the makeover to come, the hours sitting thigh-to-thigh at Matt's computer showing him her *stuff.*

Oh, dear.

She'd handle it like they did it in AA: One twinge at a time.

3

THE VOLLEYBALL tournament sign-up was at a table on the beachside terrace of a bar called WHIM SIM, short for What Happens in Malibu, Stays in Malibu.

"You lookin' to get on a team?" asked a hot guy, motioning them over. "Cuz we need a couple players."

"Absolutely," she said.

"I'm Carter." He grinned, extended his hand to Candy and gave her an appreciative once-over. He was very tanned and his hair was a sun-bleached blond that would cost a fortune in a salon, but Candy bet he'd earned it with real ray time.

"I'm Candy and this is Matt."

"Cool." Carter shook Matt's hand.

"These guys are in?" a gorgeous blonde in a red bikini, as tanned as Carter, asked. When he nodded, she beamed. "Perfect. We need two players. I'm Jaycee." She was talking to Matt and she flipped her long hair over one shoulder in an obviously practiced move.

Candy figured this was a good social moment to start Matt's lessons, so she asked Jaycee and Carter how they knew each other. Jaycee, it turned out, managed a health club in Santa Monica where Carter was a trainer. Candy explained that she and Matt worked together at SyncUp.

"You market software, huh?" Jaycee asked Matt, clearly flirting with him. "When I see 'auto run,' that's what I want to do. What kind of software do you sell?"

"We're most known for our integrated suite of applications for word processing, numerical analysis and data management."

"Sounds interesting." Jaycee's eyes glazed over.

"What Matt means is we help businesses manage their books, handle payroll, do project planning and scheduling. Like that."

"I get it. We have a payroll program, for sure. Don't know if it's yours, but the time cards take forever. No offense."

"Really?" Candy asked, her marketer's ears perking. "What would make it easier for you?"

"Fewer screens. God. It's tab, type, tab, type, tab until you want to scream."

"So, if the software could plug in routine entries for you, that would help?"

"Oh, yeah. That would be great."

"That's our job. To solve customer problems like that. Actually, Matt could get lots more technical if he wanted to. He started out as a computer engineer."

"Really?" Jaycee blinked up at him. "So you wear two hats? One day you're all thinky and into numbers and the next you're, like, creative and fresh?" Blink. Blink. She was pretending to be dumber than she clearly was.

"I don't write code these days. I manage our marketing division." There was a beat, then Matt seemed to grasp the need to keep talking. "However, my engineering background does help me interpret for both the programmers and the marketing staff."

"So you're, like, the translator. *Sprechen Sie* computer?"

"In a sense, yes." He smiled.

"That's very cool," Jaycee said. "So what are you cooking up at the moment?"

"We have a variety of projects in R & D and beta." He glanced at Candy, who urged him on with her eyes. "Uh, one you might be interested in is a personality test to help employers ensure applicants are suited to the job."

"Another test to fail." Carter groaned in pretend misery. Candy pegged him as one of those lighthearted, physical guys who were tireless in bed and eager to please their partners. Under other circumstances, he'd be the perfect companion for a week at Malibu. Too bad she was otherwise occupied.

"Yeah, but those test questions are so obvious," Jaycee said. "'Would you rather rob a liquor store or play poker with your mother?'"

"Actually," Matt said, "the test has been certified to have construct and concurrent validity, as well as—"

Candy cleared her throat.

Matt glanced at her, then paused. "Uh, basically the test measures what it claims to measure." He'd caught on, she was pleased to see. *Can the jargon.*

"Right," Candy said. "Plus, employers consider other factors when they hire."

"Like charm and good looks?" Carter said, winking at Candy.

"As long as you're qualified for the job," she teased back.

"Oh, I'm qualified." He held her gaze for a telling moment. "You two here for the festival?" He was assessing their romantic status, she could tell.

"Partly," she said. "We're doing that photo scavenger hunt, for one thing, since Matt's also a photographer." She figured that could lead to more conversation.

"That's so cool," Jaycee said. "Do you do head shots? Because I need some for my modeling composite."

"Not really. I just play around."

"You do? You play around? I *like* that."

"It's only a hobby." Matt seemed oblivious to Jaycee's flirtation.

"But he has a great eye," Candy said.

"Even better."

Lord, could the girl be more obvious? Candy felt a pang of irritation, but pushed on. "Why don't you take a snapshot of our team, Matt?"

"With the phone? Ah. Sure. Good idea." He cut her a glance that told her he knew where she was heading— get contact info.

Jaycee called over the other two players, then planted herself in the center of the picture. She was so damned *bouncy.* Like an overage high school cheerleader. Candy wasn't sure why that annoyed her, except that she seemed to be deliberately jiggling her breasts under Matt's nose.

Matt snapped the shot, then keyed e-mail addresses into his phone, finishing just as their team was called to play.

"You're a good student," she murmured to him as they headed onto the court.

"Because I have a great teacher." He held her gaze for an extra beat, giving her that melting feeling again. Between the sun and Matt, she'd be a puddle in the sand before long.

Checking out their opposing team, Candy felt intimidated. They looked so athletic. She was reasonably coordinated, but still… She glanced at Matt who smiled, calm and reassuring.

As the game went on, Matt kept his eye on her, backing her play when the sun blinded her or she was out of position when a ball came over. He even saved her shot when Radar lunged onto the court and nearly knocked her down. Matt was a strong and graceful player…who distracted the hell out of her, standing there—tall, bare-chested and gorgeous. He had to do a million pushups when he wasn't at his keyboard. Not to mention sit-ups.

She was so busy watching the way he crouched—arms extended, hands fisted together, muscles rippling—that it took her a heartbeat to notice he'd set the ball to her.

At the last second, she managed an inelegant one-armed swing and was amazed when the ball made it over the net. It surprised the other team, too, and they missed it.

Candy had earned a point by ogling Matt.

Carter slapped her on the back. "Excellent," he said, lingering near her. She noticed Matt watching the moment, pensive, slightly frowning.

The two sides traded the lead over and over, until it was game point and Candy's serve. Yikes. She moved into position, dizzy and freaked, her nerves tight as guitar strings. All eyes were on her. This one counted. She shot a look at Matt.

"It's just another serve," he murmured. "Show them what you're made of."

She would. She'd show the players. And she'd show Matt. Her ideas, that is, as soon as she got the chance. She'd show her family, too. She'd show everyone. Pumped with adrenaline and determination, she swung the ball into the air, hauled off and slugged it—straight over everyone's heads and yards out of bounds down the beach.

"Outside!" the ref called.

No kidding. Her second try went sideways and out, losing the serve for her team. Radar fetched the ball, dropping it at her feet. She tossed it over the net to the other team.

"No big thing," Matt said to her, waiting until she looked at him. "Really, Candy. It's nothing."

She felt terrible, though, and determined to make up for her failure. When her team got the serve again, the return ball came over at a tough angle. No way would she let this go without a fight, so she dived for the sand, scraping palms and knees, but managing to set the ball high.

From the ground, she watched Matt spike the ball hard.

The other team didn't have a chance.

They'd won. Her team cheered, the ref whistled for the teams to change sides, and Matt held out his hand to help her to her feet.

She smiled and reached up, enjoying the pressure of

his broad palm, his firm grip, the power in his arms. Bouncing to her feet, she rocked into him.

His arms went instinctively around her, reminding her of the moment when he'd tried to steady her before she fell anyway.

"Great dive," he said softly.

"Great spike. We make a good team."

They stood that way, eyes locked, breathing unevenly, braced in each other's arms. The seconds stretched and sagged, as sweet and slow as pulled taffy. She could feel Matt's heart beat against her hands. There was something they had to do, but she couldn't... quite...remember...what...it was.

"Hello?" Jaycee called from the other side of the net. "We're over here. New game?"

"Oh. Right." Matt jolted forward.

"You okay? Need some water?" Jaycee asked him when he reached her, extending her water bottle.

"I'm fine."

Jaycee bounced back to her position and Candy leaned toward Matt. "She wants to have your baby."

"What are you talking about?" He looked at Jaycee. "You're exaggerating."

"You should go for it."

"No. I'm not... No." He colored, embarrassed or flattered or both. A jealous prickle moved along Candy's nerves. Which was crazy. If her help juiced Matt's love life, then so much the better, right?

The game started and, again, the teams traded the lead, passing game point over and over again. Matt and Candy played together well and she managed a few good shots. In the end, they were once again victorious, which meant they took the match 2-0.

Carter, as team captain, handed out the winner's booty—a wad of drink tickets and a voucher for points in a competition that was part of the festival, along with a WHIM SIM T-shirt. "We're going inside to spend these," he said to Candy, holding up his drink coupons. "You coming?"

"Wouldn't miss it," she said.

"See you inside then." Carter turned to go.

"You like that guy?" Matt asked nodding at him.

"What's not to like?"

"He's kind of muscle-bound, don't you think? Definitely not your intellectual equal."

"Maybe that's not where I want him to be equal," she said, watching Carter enter the bar. This *was* the *Sin on the Beach* festival. It would be almost criminal not to have *some* fun. Carter had a happy-to-please boyish way about him. An all-around good-time playmate. She became aware of Matt's stare. "What?"

"Nothing. Just watching you watch him." Was that sarcasm? Maybe he felt a little jealous, too. Hmm.

"Shall we hit the bar?" she said. "We can make it another sociability lesson—see how many people you can meet."

"You're the boss," he said, brushing the sand from his legs, then his chest and arms. She imagined those hands on her, brushing sand from all those pesky places....

Stop that now. "Put this on," she said, handing him the WHIM SIM T-shirt. Enough with the bare chest already. She put on her blouse and tied it at her waist.

The T-shirt was tight on Matt and hugged every muscle and dip on his torso, making it no help at all.

She pulled her gaze away and headed for the bar. They'd have one drink and then she'd show Matt her work. That meant no booze for her. She'd stick with club soda. Mentally patting herself on the back for her good sense, she pushed open the rough-wood door to find utter drunken chaos.

The place was packed and noisy with pounding rock and drunken laughter, which swelled and subsided like ocean waves. Three women wearing bikinis danced on the massive mahogany bar. Guys on stools bellowed and whistled at them.

Down the way, a bartender in the staff uniform of a blue Hawaiian shirt passed a lighter over three liqueur shots, which burst into wavering flames. Blue martinis, the bar's signature drink, were half price, so blue liquor gleamed from martini glasses at nearly every table.

"Wow," Matt said, turning to her. He'd changed from dark glasses to regular ones before they walked in and she noticed that his eyes matched the bar's martinis. "It's pretty wild in here."

"It's summer at the beach. Time to bust out. For these people anyway." She tried not to sound sad. She itched to join the fun.

"Come on." Matt guided her to the bar and found a place inches from the tipsy dancers grinding away above them. He glanced up, then down. "Interesting," he said politely. "What would you like to drink?" He surveyed the menu overhead where specials were written in pink and green neon.

"Club soda with lime," she said grimly.

"How about we try the Tsunami for Two?"

She read the ingredients—crème de cacao, blue curaçao, rum, vodka and a bunch of juices to mask the booze. Guaranteed to make you karaoke drunk. She could even see a karaoke setup on the stage at the far side of the bar. "I don't think so. Too intense. We're working later." She felt like a complete deadbeat saying such a thing in a place like this.

"Come on. When in Rome, huh? We can 'work' tomorrow." He made quote marks around *work*. He thought she was joking.

That sent a surge of irritation through her. "It's your funeral." She would stick with her plan no matter what.

Before long, they sat at a round table barely big enough to hold the gigantic froufrou drink Matt had ordered. It was in a ceramic boat shaped like a hollowed-out tree trunk filled with blue liquid with whipped-cream whitecaps.

Matt looked down at the sea of booze. "Whose idea was this, anyway?"

"The Romans?" She gulped half her club soda, which was refreshing after so much exercise in the sun.

Matt sipped from the long, red straw at his end. "It's sweet," he said. "Thirst-quenching. Try it."

She leaned in for a sip of her straw. Fruit masked enough booze to turn a straight man into a stripper. "I think I'll stick with soda. You should pace yourself. Drink some water…"

Matt was studying her face. "Looks like you got some—" He reached out.

"Whipped cream?" She rubbed her nose to get it off.

"No, no. Sun. You've got a bit of a burn on your nose."

She laughed. "I guess after that night with the prickly-pear margaritas, I expect whenever we drink together I'll end up with something on my face." *And my legs in the air.*

"I'm not usually such a gorilla," he said, grimacing.

"And I'm not clumsy. Usually."

"I know you're not." His words had an undertone of heat that made goose bumps rise all over her body.

"So we both got the wrong impression that night," she said.

"Evidently." He looked relieved, too, and some of her embarrassment over the Tiger-Thong Incident faded.

She scooped a bit of whipped cream from their drink boat and licked it off her finger. "Mmm."

She heard Matt suck in his breath and her gaze shot to him. Licking was a suggestive thing to do. She stopped with the tip of her tongue at the middle of her upper lip. "Sorry."

"Don't be. It was…nice." He sighed, still watching her.

"So, how badly am I burned?" she asked him.

"Not too badly here." He touched the tip of her nose with a cool finger. "Check your shoulders."

She pushed her blouse down her arms and craned to see. "Maybe I should get SPF 60," she said, but when she looked at Matt he wore the strangest expression.

"Anything over 45 is a waste," he said faintly. "Most sunscreens only block UVB rays. The real damage is done by UVA rays, except avobenzone isn't yet available in the U.S., so—" He stopped. "Too much information, huh?"

"No, it's good to know. Do you think I'll blister?" She tilted a shoulder at him.

He touched her skin, sending a tingle through her that had nothing to do with her sunburn. "Doesn't look like it. No." He dropped his fingers to the table.

In the dim light, he looked a little dangerous in the black T-shirt that fit him like a second skin with his bad-boy chip and his intense gaze. Also, his inner calm and confidence. She'd bet he was an attentive lover, who took his time. With every…little…body part… Mmm.

Not what she should be thinking about right now. She had a job to do. Time to get to it. "So, networking…" she said. "We should get on that."

Matt blew out a breath. "Okay. Where do we start?"

"The idea is to expand your circle of contacts, meet as many people as you can. The more you meet, the more likely you'll find people who want our products."

"I get the theory. It's the logistics that stump me."

"The secret is open-ended questions. Talk less, listen more. Any answer you get should lead to another question. People love to be listened to. As you talk, you'll discover what you have in common and develop rapport. Naturally, you work around to business topics, product needs and stuff like that."

"You make it sound easy."

"It is. Once you get the hang of it. I'll demonstrate."

She started up a conversation with the couple at the next table about the blue martinis they were drinking, ending with an invitation to visit SyncUp, since the pair turned out to be communications majors at UCLA.

When it was over, Matt grinned at her. "You're

amazing. Another minute and they'd have asked you to be a bridesmaid in their wedding."

She laughed, warmed by his praise.

"How did you learn this, anyway?" he asked.

"Some of it's instinct, but I practice. Also, I've been going on client visits with one of our customer liaisons, picking up customer interests and ideas."

"I didn't know you did that."

"There's lots you don't know about me," she said, advancing her cause, she hoped.

"I imagine so," he said softly, studying her. She couldn't tell what he was thinking, but she had a feeling it was more personal than professional.

"Anyway, now it's your turn to try. If we were at a convention, I'd challenge you to collect twenty business cards."

"I doubt many of these people carry cards," Matt said, watching two girls in bikinis walk by.

"So collect phone numbers."

"Won't the women think I'm coming on to them?"

"Not if you give off a business vibe. Or you could just talk to the men."

"So *they* can think I'm coming on to them?"

She laughed. "No man with functional gaydar would think you're playing for the other team."

"It's because I don't layer, isn't it?" He pretended to be sad, shaking his head in false gloom.

"Definitely," she joked, not willing to dwell on the details of his masculinity. "We'll fix that tomorrow."

"Uh-oh," Matt said.

"Relax. I promise it will be as painless as possible."

"I'm in your hands."

Don't I wish. A sigh escaped her and Matt's eyes locked on.

"What the hell is that?"

They both jolted at the interruption. Jaycee was pointing at the booze boat, then crouched beside Matt so her breasts bulged up at him like grapefruit fighting for air.

"It's a Tsunami for Two." Matt held out his straw and Jaycee sipped, leaning forward to emphasize her cleavage. Gentleman that he was, Matt kept his gaze trained on her face.

"Yum," she said, smacking her lips. An old Cars tune rocked through the bar. "Want to dance?" she asked him.

"I can't dance," Matt said, shrugging.

"After that, you can." She nodded at the Tsunami.

"Candy and I are talking business."

Jaycee looked askance.

"It can wait," Candy said. "Go on, Matt." If he got busy with Jaycee, that would be a surefire end to Candy's fixation.

"Maybe later," he said to Jaycee.

She shrugged—*your loss*—then bounded back to her table, not wounded at all.

"You could have gone," Candy said in case Matt was trying to be chivalrous. "I'd be fine on my own."

"I'm sure you would be," he said, "but we're working, right? Isn't that what you wanted?" He held her gaze, then seemed to catch himself and ducked down to take a long pull on his straw. "This tastes better and better."

"Maybe you should give it a rest. Want some?" She tilted her club soda at him.

"I'm fine," he said, waving her away, drinking deeply from the booze boat. "I feel more like slapping backs with every swallow. How many phone numbers should I get, coach?"

"We should make it interesting. Maybe a competition? See which of us can meet the most people?"

"You're too good. You'll win hands down."

"I'll give myself a handicap…say I get two for every one you get. How's that?"

"Sounds fair. What are the stakes?"

"Let me think about that for a while." She should come up with something they'd both want.

A roar rose as a woman was passed over the top of a group of guys, then lowered to the floor.

"It's kind of crazy in here," Matt said. "Maybe we should find another place."

"You have to seize the moment. You never know where a contact will come from." She watched five guys drop shots into beer mugs and guzzle them. Matt may have a point.

"Hey, lady. You, me, there!" Carter pointed at her, then him, then the dance floor.

She looked at Matt.

"Go on," he said. "I've got this to finish." He motioned at the Tsunami.

"I wouldn't, if I were you," she said, but Carter had led her too far away to be heard over the noise.

On the crowded dance floor, Carter rested his hands lightly on her hips for the slowish song. She looked over at Matt, who was sucking down his drink way too fast.

"So, what are you doing after this?" Carter asked.

"Huh?" She looked at him. "After this?"

"Yeah. After this." He was clearly interested in spending more time with her, but with Matt around, she didn't dare risk anything that might reinforce her party-girl image.

"Working," she said sadly.

He looked at her questioningly.

"Really," she said on a sigh. She glanced toward Matt just as a curvy brunette in a teensy bikini was leading him to the floor. That was a surprise.

When they were close enough, Matt leaned toward Candy. "I'll be getting her number," he said, sounding a bit boozy. The Tsunami seemed to have reached land.

He turned to his partner, who promptly wiggled down his body, freak style, then up again. Matt's eyes went wide and he froze.

Candy almost burst out laughing. The girl turned her back, bent forward and rubbed her bottom in a deliberate circle against his crotch.

Matt looked at Candy over the woman's bent body and shrugged, hands up.

"When in Rome!" she called to him. She could rescue him, but first she'd see how he handled this on his own.

4

WHAT THE HELL AM I supposed to do now? Matt wondered, as his partner rolled her ass around and around against his groin.

He would never have stepped onto the dance floor if Steroid Steve didn't have his hands all over Candy. He didn't want to look like a total loser sucking down a froufrou drink while she rocked the dance floor.

Now this girl was having mock sex with him in front of God and the entire bar. He didn't even know her name, let alone her number. Thank God he was too shocked to be erect.

She didn't seem to care what he did, moving around as though this was a *dance* with actual *steps,* though her feet stayed in place. Her hips and ass and breasts were doing all the work.

She was stylin', moving her arms just so, her attention focused inward, oblivious to him. He was only a prop for her gyrations. Now she faced him, her leg between his, and slid down his body, as if he were a chrome pole.

Meanwhile, Candy, who could make him hard as stone by running her tongue across her lips, was laughing at him. She thought a strange woman humping him was hilarious.

Actually, it was pretty funny.

In a few seconds, Candy danced Carter over and arranged a partner trade. The muscle-bound Carter appeared happy to grind away with Matt's partner, who didn't mind the switch either, it seemed. Whatever spun your hard drive, he guessed.

Speaking of which, Candy was now inches away from him, swaying her tight body to the music. She grinned up at him. "You should have seen your face. You looked paralyzed."

"I thought she'd start on my zipper any second."

"Would that have been so bad?" she asked, teasing him, her eyes brimming with laughter. "What happens in Malibu, stays in Malibu, remember?"

A much slower song began, so, of course, he had to put his arms around her. She rested her palms lightly on his shoulders, keeping her lower body a discreet distance away.

He was glad, since he was mortifyingly erect. Around Candy, he felt sixteen and defenseless against his parts.

The crowd shifted abruptly and someone knocked Candy into him. Now she would feel his…*yep*. Her face told him she'd noticed his hard-on.

"Sorry," he muttered.

"Don't apologize," she said shakily. "You had a woman rubbing on you. Of course you're going to—"

"It wasn't her," he said, holding her gaze, letting her see the truth, something he'd never have done if he'd been thinking straight. But Candy and the Tsunami for Two had addled his brain.

"Oh." Candy took that in, exhaled, and seemed to

melt even closer to him. They stayed that way, bodies pressed together, pretending the crowd had forced them into such close contact.

He rested his hands on the curves of her swaying hips, pressing lightly with his fingers, keeping his groin against hers. The laundry-list of liquors in that zippy blue boat he'd just guzzled rushed along his bloodstream, relaxing him into this cheat. Dancing was a legitimate reason to hold her close. And she felt so good to him.

Maybe it wasn't booze, just testosterone—the flood brought on by Candy—that washed away all his good sense.

They looked at each other, bodies tight together, her breasts pressed into his chest, pelvis-to-groin, moving in effortless rhythm.

"How are you doing?" Candy asked.

"Better now," he said. *Holding you.* He wanted to slide his hands down to her ass, grip her hard and kiss her mindless.

"You look dazed," she said, smiling.

He *was* dazed. By her and how much he wanted her. That seemed lame, so he said, "I guess I am. This place is not my scene." Around them drunks bellowed, hooted and poured beer on each other. Women were dancing on the bar. A few danced on tables, one girl in just a bra and panties. "I'm glad I've got an experienced guide."

Her eyes went dark, as if he'd insulted her. "As your guide, I suggest you pace yourself on that Tsunami."

"Too late. I polished it off." And he was feeling it, too.

"What am I going to do with you?" She shook her head, as if he were a kid who'd overdone it with the birthday cake.

He was a charity case to her, he realized. The networking lessons and tomorrow's makeover were her attempt to rescue him from terminal dorkdom. That sucked.

To distract himself from that gloomy idea, he danced closer to the crowd forming near the stage. A sign above a table announced a karaoke contest and people seemed to be signing up.

"Those poor idiots," Matt said. He wouldn't be caught dead singing in public, not even drunk.

"You know, I always thought SyncUp should create karaoke software," Candy said. "What's missing is good background videos so it feels like a real performance, don't you think?"

"I suppose." He considered the idea, studying the stage, wondering about rear projection and stock footage, possible markets, development costs....

He was so preoccupied that he didn't notice Candy had moved away until she was back. Grinning.

Uh-oh. Dread filled him. "You didn't do what I think you did, did you?"

"I signed us up for a duet!" She beamed triumphantly.

"Yeah, but I was the silent bass player, remember?"

"You'll be fine. I'll carry us. We're doing 'You're the One That I Want.' From *Grease?* I was in the musical in high school."

"So, I'm supposed to be John Travolta? God."

"You'll do great."

He should back out, he knew, but he didn't want to

disappoint her. She'd made him feel as though he could dance. She could probably make him feel as though he could sing, too. Candy made him want to let go, let whatever happened, happen.

Well, Candy and that massive tiki drink.

The first few performers weren't bad. A couple of 'faced frat boys sang "Shout." A trio of girls sang a Bangles song. And a guy with a huge cowboy hat wobbled through a sad country tune.

When it was their turn, Matt's gut twisted with anxiety, but he led Candy to the stage, forcing a smile. He found that if he closed one eye, he could just about read the lyrics from the prompter.

The song kicked off and Candy carried him, just as she'd promised, her voice clear and crisp and perfectly in tune. She danced around him in a way that seemed choreographed. For his part, he managed a well-timed dip here and there.

She sang the chorus—the title of the song—right at him, her eyes bright, her face glowing, her body warm in his arms.

He was overheated, buzzed from the booze, and all he wanted to do was stay on this stupid stage singing away, just to hold her a while longer.

He sang the chorus and realized he meant the words. And for a beat of time, he saw in her eyes that she meant them, too.

The song ended and the crowd applauded wildly, whistling and bellowing and pounding the tables. He helped Candy off the stage, shaken by what he'd felt. They watched the rest of the performers, arms at each other's waists, glancing at each other from time to time, not speaking. She seemed as startled as he.

After the last singer, they were called up with the other contestants so the crowd could choose the winner by drunken applause.

He wasn't surprised when the audience went nuts for them. It was all Candy, he knew, and they walked away with the grand prize, a trophy shaped like a microphone, ten free dinners-for-two at a Santa Monica restaurant and a voucher for five hundred festival points. Whatever that was.

Once they were off stage, Candy threw her arms around his neck. "We did it, Matt! We won!"

"It was all you." The title of the song said it all. His desire for her thundered through him, overpowering what was left of his inhibitions and he decided to kiss her. He leaned over and—

Candy jerked back, surprised. She looked left, then patted the speaker on a stand beside them. "Just making sure I wasn't about to knock it over."

She was easing the tension with a joke, he could tell, so he went along. "That was my fault. I knocked you down." He cringed at the memory of his oafish move.

"No, sir. You tried to keep me from falling. It was my fault. I thought you wanted to kiss me, so I reached up."

"I *was* trying to kiss you."

"But there was margarita on my chin."

"An excuse."

"Too bad it didn't work out." Her breathing was uneven and her eyes flew across his face, unsure whether to run or stay.

"I always regretted I didn't get to show you my moves," he joked, but his throat was dry and he was sweating buckets.

"You have moves?" Her words were breathless.

Without another thought, he lowered his mouth to hers.

A quiver passed through her body, then she held very still. He went for her tongue and she made a soft sound and let go, her body sagging so that he had to hold her up.

The crowd roared around him, his blood pulsed in his ears and all he wanted was Candy's sweet mouth.

It was crazy, he knew, but at the moment, good sense was just so much white noise in his head. They wobbled together, almost tipping over. He didn't care. He'd take the speaker out this time if he had to. He wasn't letting go of Candy until they were done.

MATT'S KISS WENT FROM playful to hot like *that*. Candy felt as though she'd leaned in for a sip from a water fountain and gotten a blast from a fire hose. She could barely stand and couldn't breathe at all.

She held the karaoke trophy in one hand and wrapped the other around Matt's neck, holding on tight, fighting to keep from falling, wanting more of Matt's mouth, his tongue, feeling his erection against her body, his fingers on her bottom.

She heard moans, too. Low, desperate sounds they were both making, a sweet duet of heat and need.

She wanted to crawl clear inside the man.

Matt was drunk, not himself, to be kissing her this wildly in public. So what was her excuse?

It was how much he wanted her. His fierce kiss made

her woozy and weak. Her sex was so tight she thought it might snap—she hoped it would to ease the agony she felt.

In the background, music pounded and people yelled and laughed and carried on, wild for a good time. She and Matt were smack-dab in the spirit of things, surfing this wave of heedless pleasure….

Until a cold trickle of good sense drizzled into her awareness. Making out in a bar was pure party girl, a page from her PQ2 report. Her job—hell, her future—was on the line.

She'd learned that lesson, hadn't she? Sex at work was a bad idea. Look at what happened to her reputation after she kissed poor Jared. She had to put the brakes on. Now.

She managed to pry her lips away and grab Matt's shoulders. "You…don't…want…this," she said between gasps.

"Oh, yes, I do," he said, pulling her back by her ass.

"You're drunk, Matt."

"Not that drunk." He hiccuped. "What stays in Malibu, happens in Malibu… Er, whatever happens, stays… You know what I mean."

"If you can't even say it, you can hardly do it." She backed away, giving herself space. "At least not with me. Try Jaycee, Matt." She searched the bar for the bouncy blonde.

"I don't want Jaycee. I want you." His eyes grabbed her and held on. The words from their song vibrated in her head. Insane and stupid and pointless.

"Let's get some air," she said, pushing out of his arms, starting toward the door.

Matt grabbed her by the waist to guide her through the crowd, which had become denser by the minute.

As soon as they got outside, Matt pulled her to him. "I need your mouth." Having this no-nonsense engineer so hot for her was such a rush, but she knew it was wrong.

"What you need is to sleep it off," she said, breaking away. She'd never before said no to something she wanted this badly. "Let's walk," she said shakily, needing a distraction. She shoved the trophy into her bag and kicked off her sandals.

Matt gave in, took her hand and led her toward the ebbing tide. A light breeze lifted her hair and cooled her body.

The sea looked like polished silver beneath the pale orange and pink of the blooming sunset, which gave the air an otherworldly glow. A few sailboats rode the breeze along the horizon.

"I feel *sooo* good tonight," Matt said, leaning back to look up at the sky. He staggered a little and she laughed.

"And you'll feel *sooo* bad tomorrow."

"It was worth it. I never let loose like this." Then he muttered, as if to himself, "Jane was right about me."

"Your girlfriend?"

"Did Ellie tell you about Jane?"

"In passing, yes." She didn't want Matt to know Ellie told her every detail she knew.

"Well, Jane claims I don't know how to relax."

"Really?"

He nodded, wearing a half-assed grin. "Her exact words were, 'You wouldn't know fun if it threw you a surprise party.'"

"Ouch. That's harsh."

"Espe-shly coming from someone who works jus' as hard." He was slurring and now he squinted, as if to compensate for double vision. "She's a lawyer. Sixty-hour weeks *eeeeasy*. We had that in common. We're both career oriented and goal driven."

"You sound like a corporation," she said.

"Yeah. True." He nodded a couple of times. "Thatz what made us a good match. Bu' I was wrong." He sighed and shook his head. "She broke up with me."

He's still in love with her. Candy felt a jolt of disappointment. But this was helpful, she knew. Matt still loved Jane. Like garlic to werewolves, this would ward off Candy's own lust, keep her from imagining things that could never be.

Things she didn't even want, for Pete's sake.

"Being here with you is good for me," Matt said now, throwing an arm around her shoulder. "You're showing me how to be…what did you say? 'Fun Guy.' Yeah. I could get into that. I've been missing out…a lot." He tried to turn her toward him, to embrace her, she was sure.

She scooted away.

He was so tough to resist. His eyes were soft, but still hot, moving over her body, wanting her, no longer able to politely look away from her breasts, her hips, her mouth.

She had to stay in charge. "I bet when Jane sees Fun Guy, she'll want you back, Matt."

"She won't believe iz me, tha'z for sure." He chuckled. They walked a little farther. "So, whadowe do now?" he asked her. "Back to my place? For a drink?"

Bad, bad idea. "I was supposed to show you my ideas on Ledger Lite, but you're in no shape for that. How about we start early in the morning? Before we go to the mall? I'll borrow your computer so I can get organized tonight."

"If you say so," he said, shaking his head. "I can't believe you wanna work."

They made it to his place and he invited her in again, his eyes offering more than the Cheetos and HoHos he was trying to tempt her with.

"Just the computer," she said, standing firm outside his door.

"Okay. You're one tough cookie," he said, giving up and going to get his computer. He put the case's strap over her shoulder. "There you go."

"Is seven-thirty too early to come back?" she asked.

"I'm up at six." He tilted his head at her. "Do you know how remarkable you are?" He was looking her over as if she were dessert. The booze had melted away all traces of politeness.

"That's the Tsunami talking, Matt, but thanks."

"See you in the morning, then."

When he leaned out to kiss her, she chastely gave him her cheek, but she greedily inhaled the warm, human smell of him—salt and man and lime. Matt.

She headed to her place, computer snug at her side. She was proud of herself. She'd fought off the ache to get naked with Matt and stuck to her mission.

It was only 7:00. She had plenty of time to key in her notes, consolidate e-mails and leave a voice mail for Freeda, who worked 7:00 to 3:00 and could nab

Candy's hard-drive files for her in the morning before she went to Matt's.

If only her family could see her now. Though the proof would be the promotion. That would be tangible evidence of her success. The promotion would redeem her, prove her maturity, make her respectable in their eyes. She was making definite progress. Tomorrow, Matt would see what a good team leader she would make. This was working out just fine, despite the Tsunami-inspired make-out.

At the beach house, Candy was delighted to find Sara and Ellie stretched out on the foldout couch Candy would sleep on. Both were sucking on BombPops, the red, white and blue Popsicles she remembered from her childhood, and laughing at TV.

"Hey, Candy, what have you been up to?" Ellie asked.

"Working with Matt." She grinned, proud that it was true.

"No way. All this time?"

"Every minute." The hardest work of all had been walking away. She sank into a chair beside the bed, happy to be with her friends, vowing not to confess her close call.

"Your nose is burned," Sara said. "And what's that sticking out of your bag?"

Candy held up the trophy. "We won this in a karaoke contest. Matt and I sang a duet. It was work, believe it or not. Before that we won our game in this volleyball tournament. Also work, because—"

"Hold it right there," Ellie said, raising her hand in a stop sign. "You got my brother to sing? In front of a crowd?"

She shrugged.

Ellie squealed and tapped her Popsicle against Sara's. "I told you they would hook up."

"We didn't hook up." Though they'd come damn close. "We made this deal about work. My computer croaked, so he's loaning me his. In exchange, I'm helping him with his social skills, which he has to improve because of his PQ2 scores."

"Matt gave up his laptop?" Ellie said. "That's amazing. He's, like, hooked by umbilical to it."

"Exactly. It's part of helping him be more social. He was very impressed with my networking skills."

"Your *networking* skills?" Sara grinned.

"So, you made a deal to teach Matt how to party?" Ellie said. "That is so *you*." She saluted Candy with her BombPop.

"It's not that way." Except she saw how it might seem so. "Anyway, I'm going over there tomorrow morning to work." She had to change the subject. "So what have you two been up to?"

She spotted Sara's computer on the counter, still on. "You didn't work after we talked?"

"Just a little," Sara said.

"She took a break long enough to meet a hot guy, though," Ellie said, "until Uncle Spence called and ruined it."

"Sara, if I can work on vacation, you can try not to."

"I *am* trying," Sara said with a heavy sigh.

The girls talked on about the guy Sara had met—he owned a surf shop and Ellie thought Sara needed lessons—and then Ellie had news about an audition for extras for *Sin on the Beach*.

"And here's the best part," Sara said. "The director is a guy she knew from when she was a kid."

"No!"

"He was our next-door neighbor when I was twelve. Bill Romero—eighteen and *sooo* hot. I wrote about him in my diary, fantasized about my first kiss with him— my first, well, everything. I only spoke to him once and that was to ask if he was really going to film school in New York. He was and that was that. He left and my heart shattered into a million pieces."

"And that's what sent you to the dark side?" Candy asked. "You started in with the vampires and the undead?"

"Oh, stop."

"So, do you have an in with the show? Because of Bill?"

"He didn't recognize me. Of course, back then I wore overalls all the time and my hair was flyaway and mousy brown."

"So now he can fall for the grown-up Ellie," Candy said.

"Hardly," Ellie said.

In the silence, Candy noticed the boom-chica-boom soundtrack coming from the TV. "What are you two watching?"

"*Summer Sluts,* I think it's called," Ellie said. "We're getting Sara in the mood for her surf guy. With these, too." She lifted the ice pop. "We're picking up oral techniques." Ellie gave her Popsicle an exaggerated lick.

"How does she do that?" Sara asked, watching one of the video sluts bend backward off the side of the bed.

"Her spine's made of whatever Gumby is," Ellie declared.

"They make it look easy," Sara said with a sigh.

"They make it look fake," Candy said. There was no emotion, no energy, no heat. Nothing like the incredible melting desire she'd felt in Matt's arms.

"Hey…" Sara said. Candy glanced over to find Sara staring at her. "What's *up* with you? You're all pink and glowing."

"It's just the sunburn." Candy was no poker player, so she deflected the conversation. "What time's the audition, El?"

"Gak! The crack of dawn. Seven o'clock. Can you believe that? I'll sleep through, no doubt. When I'm not at the coffee bar, I'm never up before noon."

"I'll get you up, no problem," Sara said.

"Courtesy of an Uncle Spence call?" Candy asked.

Sara shrugged. She obviously hadn't made much headway in her plan to run free of her demanding uncle.

"I doubt I'll make the cut," Ellie said. "Goth is not a beach-babe look."

"Oh, but we can fix that, can't we, Sara?" Candy climbed onto the bed and looked Ellie over. "Maybe soften your contrasts. Let's see…" She fingered Ellie's black curls. "We could straighten your hair…give it sun streaks."

"Are you crazy?" Ellie grabbed both sides of her hair.

"Only temporarily, of course," Candy said, winking at Sara. "We wouldn't want the Queen of the Damned to look too cheerful."

"There's Walgreens up the way for the color and straightener," Sara said. "And we can use my makeup.

Pastel shadow to bring out your eyes. Bronzer so you're not so pale."

"Then all you need is the right bikini," Candy said, getting into the makeover idea. Matt tomorrow and Ellie tonight.

"How about my black one?" Sara said. "It's cut high."

"Perfect. Absolutely sinful."

"This is too much fuss over me," Ellie said.

"It's about time," Candy said. "This vacation is about breaking out of old patterns. You're always doing things for us. Let us return the favor."

"Exactly," Sara said, wiping a cherry drip from a flyer on the coffee table. It was the same puce as the one at Matt's place. "And look at this. There's a contest as part of the festival." She held the flyer so they could read. "You get points for events. The grand prize is a month-long time-share at a beach condo here for ten years."

"So that's what the vouchers were for," Candy said. "Matt and I got five hundred points for the karaoke win and another two hundred for the volleyball game."

"I think there was something about getting festival points for auditioning," Ellie mused. "Double if you get a part."

"That's great," Sara said. "It says you can work as a team. Candy, you and Matt gave us a head start with your wins. The finalists submit an essay about why they deserve the condo."

"Candy can write that," Ellie said.

"Three good friends who need to escape from their lives for one week each year? Hell, it'll write itself." Candy grinned.

"We should divvy up events to maximize points," Sara said.

"Great idea. I can make this part of my deal with Matt. We're already doing the photo shoot."

"I'll build a spreadsheet so we can be strategic." Sara wore her efficiency-mode expression.

"Not if this means more work for you," Candy said.

"This isn't work. This is fun." Sara beamed. "If we win, we'll have a fabulous condo together every summer."

The girls high-fived each other.

"Let's hit the drugstore for Ellie's hair stuff," Sara said, jumping up.

This would be a blast, Candy thought, starting to get up. Then she caught sight of Matt's computer. She'd sworn to get organized for tomorrow. She would choose long-term gain over short-term fun. "You two go ahead. I have to work."

Her friends gawked at her.

"I'm going to his place early. I've got to prepare." She spoke sternly. After a long, shocked silence, her friends accepted her decision and left without her.

At least they hadn't laughed.

She almost went after them and bought beach toys and water blasters for good measure, but she pictured her brothers rolling their eyes. *We knew you couldn't work on vacation.*

Oh, yes she could, dammit. She turned on Matt's computer, but as it fired to life, she felt herself go dead. Bone weary. Fighting her urges all day had worn her out. She needed something to perk herself up. Coffee? Better would be a hard run along the beach and a few primal screams into the Malibu twilight.

Stripping to her bikini, she grabbed a towel, left a note for her friends, and set off running.

5

As soon as Candy left, Matt realized he was well and truly smashed. He'd been so pumped with adrenaline and testosterone around her that he hadn't truly felt the booze. He'd be sorry in the morning. She was right about that.

He tossed off his shirt and threw himself across his bed to watch the ceiling fan swirl. Then he noticed the fan wasn't on. It was the ceiling that was spinning.

He jammed his foot to the floor to still the wonky kaleidoscope overhead. He felt as though he'd been tossed on his head by a real tsunami.

It was not just the liquor. It was Candy, too. He kept thinking about how her body felt in his arms, how soft her lips were, how sweet she'd tasted.

He knew he should regret kissing her, but he only wanted more. He knew the address of Ellie's beach house. What if he moseyed over there?

Bad idea. Even drunk, he knew that. They *worked* together. He was her *boss*. And if Ellie was there to see him arrive, he'd never live it down.

He couldn't believe he'd consider such a desperate act, even drunk. On the other hand, Candy was something else. She made him think of the summer fireflies of his childhood that he'd chased with a jar to get a closer look at their magic.

Who could resist her?

Abruptly, he remembered that beach bum who'd danced with her. Carter had practically eaten her up with his eyes. *Maybe that's not where I want him to be equal,* she'd said.

Maybe she was with him right now. She wasn't the kind of girl who called it a night at 7:00.

The thought burned through him and he jumped out of bed, needing to occupy himself. He could get started on the new org chart, sketch out possible teams. He'd brought personnel thumbnails for that purpose.

Nah. His mind was too scattered. He'd go online, catch up on e-mail. He'd walked all the way to the kitchen before he remembered that Candy had his computer. Damn.

He channel surfed for a while, restless, legs jumping, skin itchy. An hour passed somehow and he found himself staring out the window at the ocean, swaying a little.

Hell, why not swim off the booze? A brisk dip would clear his head and tame his libido at the same time. He threw on his trunks, tucked his key in the mesh pocket and headed out.

The moonlit water was cool, but not brutal, and he took long, hard strokes parallel to the shore, swimming until his breath came in hard gasps. He rested in a dog paddle and checked out the horizon, squinting, since he was without his glasses. The moon created a streak of silver across the black, rolling water.

He noticed rhythmic splashes to his left and saw someone in a yellow bikini swimming straight out to sea.

Candy? She had that color suit—he'd stared at her in it all day—and the swimmer was plowing single-mindedly through the water, the way Candy took on the world.

He swam close enough to see that, sure enough, it was her. How far would she go? She was smart, but headstrong. She might exhaust herself before she realized it and not make it back. At that thought, everything in him gathered tight. If something happened to her…

He was about to go after her when she reversed course and swam his way, the water flashing silver with each stroke.

He found the reef and stood, waiting for her. When she was close enough, he called her name, which made her jerk her head out of the water and blink at him.

"Matt?" She flailed her arms, shifting into an upright dog paddle. "What are you doing here?"

"Swimming off the booze."

A gentle wave rolled by, lifting first her, then him, sliding them closer.

"Is it working?" she asked, smiling at him.

"I hope so. What brought you out here?"

"I was restless," she said, stepping onto the reef, closer to him, her chest rising and falling rapidly as she caught her breath. Her hair was sleek, her makeup gone, but she looked incredible to him.

He wanted her so much it stunned him. It was as though his desire had conjured her out of the sea, made it okay for them to be together, to do what they both felt like doing.

All the reasons why he couldn't have her slid away on the waves. Every nerve was on fire for her, every muscle strained to touch her. It was as if he'd been sleepwalking through his life and now he was awake. Wide awake. For her.

He pulled her into his arms and kissed her mouth, salty from the sea.

Her body shook against him, her lips trembled and she broke away. "You're still drunk, Matt." She searched his face.

"Not so much now." He pressed his mouth to her neck, felt her pulse wild against his lips. He returned to her mouth, heat and need flowing through him.

Candy stilled against him, filled, he was sure, with the doubts he'd let float away on the sea.

If she was serious about stopping, he'd respect that, but first he'd do his best to persuade her this was the right thing to do. Everything in him said it was.

Well, almost everything.

After a few seconds, he felt her let go, as if a cord had snapped inside, freeing her. She wrapped her legs and arms around him and kissed him back, offering her tongue, which he took, reveling in her moaning response.

The moment felt as primal as the waves that swelled and subsided around them, rocking them together with slow, inexorable power, pulling them into primal, instinctive acts, the way the moon tugged the tide.

Except Matt wanted civilization at the moment. "Let's find a bed before we drown."

Candy burst out laughing. He loved the husky sound and the way she put her whole body into it.

He lifted her up and she tucked her head under his chin, then he carried her to shore and across the sand, enjoying the weight of her against him, the way she clasped her fingers trustingly behind his neck. Desire beat time in his body, suspending all thought except how he would soon be inside her.

It seemed simultaneously to take forever and no time at all before he was unlocking his door. He moved with care over the slick entry tiles, relieved when his toes hit the carpet. He padded down the hall, paused to grab towels from the bathroom, then carried Candy to his bed.

The spread was soft, thank God, because he wasn't taking time to peel it back. He ran the towel over her body, then his, sopping up some of the seawater, then kissed her face, her neck, unhooked her top and tossed it to the floor.

There were her round breasts, their tips knotted from the cold. He cupped their firm curves, perfect handfuls, butter-soft except for the nipples, which were smooth beads against his palm.

She leaned back, making her nipples poke out, tight and eager, welcoming his tongue, his lips, his teeth for a taste, a suck, a gentle bite.

He ran his tongue around one nipple, then the other, tasting salt and skin, feeling the tiny bumps swell and subside under his pushing tongue.

She stiffened, then collapsed into quick, helpless jerks of her hips. Her hips. Yeah. That reminded him of the rest of her, which he wanted naked, too, so he dragged her bikini bottoms down. His fingers scraped sand. He brushed the grit from her tender flesh, then studied her belly. Her pulse was a series of quivering blips under her pale skin. There was a light pink line above her pubic curls from the sun they'd gotten today.

He slid out of his trunks and Candy grasped his cock, her hand warm, making his vision fade.

She explored him with slow fingers, making him harder with each sure stroke, making him push against her palm.

He ran his hands along the curve of her hip and between her thighs, which she parted so he could stroke the swollen lips of her sex, then her clitoris, slowly bearing down until a shiver of pleasure rippled through her body and she moaned, her hand stopping on his cock, she was so caught up in what he was doing to her.

They weren't speaking, only giving groans and gasps and cries of approval. This was so good. No way would he regret this.

He eased one finger into her wet velvet space.

She gasped, surprised, then bit her lip as if the pleasure were so great it almost hurt.

He moved on top of her and captured the lip she'd bit to lick it better, to taste her sweet mouth again, while his fingers explored her slick sex, pushing in slowly, then pulling out again.

She made breathy mewling sounds, lying very still, as if concentrating on his every move. Now and then she tried to stroke him, but seemed too absorbed in what he was doing.

He was happy to be making her so happy.

"You'd better...we'd better...what about a condom?" She sounded desperate.

The barrier would slow him down and he wanted to make this last. Were there any in his toiletry kit? A few from the early days with Jane, he was sure.

"When we need one, I'll get it. I'm happy here for now. You?"

"Mmm, hmm." She nodded, lips parted, breathing through her mouth. She relaxed into the bed, lying open to his fingers. Moonlight bathed her parts—her breasts, belly, hip bones, curls, her taut thighs. He memorized her—her shape, her breath, the way her tongue swept her lips and her face—reveling in how she seemed to be sinking into the moment with him.

He kissed the impossibly soft skin of her neck, ran his tongue over her pulse, stroked the button of her sex, which swelled, eager for more. His thumb in place, he slid two fingers in and out of her in a rhythm he mimicked with his mouth and wanted to begin with his cock.

Her hips rocked faster, she tightened around his fingers. "Oh, oh, oh. I'm going to—"

"Come. Yeah. Come for me."

She sped up, getting closer and closer until…

There.

She froze against the bed, then yelped, her eyes rolling back as she bucked against his finger. He felt so grateful to be with her, to feel her fire and energy and desire, to give her what she wanted.

He realized he'd sensed her needs without words. This was a surprise, this automatic understanding. It was as if they'd been together many times before.

"Oh, wow," she breathed, rolling over and onto him.

"That was—" She finished her sentence with a very wet, very violent kiss.

Abruptly, she rose to her knees and pressed his arms to the bed, looking as though she intended to wrestle him into submission.

"Uncle," he said. "Aunt and cousin, too, if that helps."

She smiled the smile of a hellcat bent on getting her due. Then she hesitated. "The condom…" She bit her lip. "I'm on the pill. I get tested. You?"

"I'm…healthy," he said, not sure how he'd even make it to the bathroom with this incredible woman above him.

"Good. Bareback it is." She guided his cock into her body, slowly seating herself at the base of his shaft, settling in with a moan of pleasure. She arched her body, head back, enjoying this, it seemed.

He certainly was. Her tight, hot sex was pure heaven. He grabbed her hips, pulling her down harder.

She looked at him, her hair falling forward, color in her cheeks, her eyes shining in the dimness. She was so beautiful.

"This just gets better, huh?" she breathed.

"Oh, yeah," he said, thrusting up into her. "Better and better." This had to be the best position. Except for looking down at her body. Or lying on his side, facing her. Or all the other positions they hadn't tried. Yet.

"Mmm." She sucked in her breath, then did a slow roll on his shaft, bending him, intensifying the rush of blood pulsing through his member. He was buried to the hilt in her. He moved in and out, rocking to press her clit with his shaft, loving the way she moaned each time.

He reached for her breasts and she bent forward so he could cup their weight and lick each nipple in turn.

She did a rolling twist with her hips that made him moan in sweet agony. He kissed her mouth, tugged at her tongue, held her breasts and lightly teased the nipples, giving her, he hoped, some of the hot rush that poured through him.

She rose to a full sit and he pressed his finger to her clit. Her head snapped forward. "Oh, yes. Do *that*." She smiled the smile of a woman galloping toward a pleasure she knew was waiting just for her. He loved that look. He wanted to see it over and over.

He pushed her clit as he pumped upward, hard.

She gasped, then tensed, as if electrified by sensation, and he knew she was coming.

He let her spasms pull him into his own release. Closing his eyes, he pulsed into her, in time with her squeezing muscles. They were together in this crackle of electricity, riding its surging pulse together.

He usually made sure his lovers came first, but this mutual pleasure had happened as easily as breathing. And so much more fun.

She flopped against his chest with a great gasp of an exhale. "Oh. Wow. That was…"

"Great," he said into her hair, which smelled of spice and flowers, her sweet sweat and the salty metal of the sea. "God, you smell great. I can't—" sniff "—get—" sniff "—enough."

He hadn't felt this way before, had he?

Maybe with Heather. Back in college. Listening to Candy catch her breath, he couldn't help thinking of his first real love. Heather had had the same wild energy as Candy. She'd had a thing for thrill rides, the more frightening the better. She'd loved sex, too, said it felt like the click-click-click to the top of the first coaster drop. She loved the anticipation, loved shrieking into the dive.

The breakup had been unexpected and painful, even though she'd warned him—laughing—that she had emotional ADD. *I never stick long.* He'd thought it would be different with him. It hadn't been.

He'd been shocked by how bad he felt and for how long and had stayed clear of women like Heather ever since.

Until Candy. He felt the uneasy rumble inside, like the distant thunder of a storm on its way. *Don't ruin this,* he told himself. *Stop thinking.* Easy enough to do with the liquor still numbing his brain. Yeah, he was still drunk.

But for now he was content to breathe in Candy. God, she smelled good.

MATT WAS TAKING big, greedy sniffs of her hair and Candy smiled at how sweet that was. She felt stunned and so grateful. She'd had her share of quality sex, but this had been something else. Effortlessly great.

She'd suspected that Matt would be hot, but not so…oh…what was the word? Aware? In tune? It was as if he inhabited her body, knew exactly where she needed the most attention and for how long, when to go faster, harder and when to hold stock-still.

And all without a word. She liked the talkers—the men who took the time to pin down what she wanted and who guided her, too, in what they preferred—but Matt was in a class by himself.

What would she call him? A body reader. Yeah. She released a huge breath, sated from two close-together orgasms, enjoying the thud of Matt's heart beneath her, the way he held her gently but securely, how their mingled sweat made them slick as seals, the way he smelled of lime and spice and sea and sex.

She'd loved how he'd swept her into his arms and carried her to the house like some dashing rogue from an old historical novel, intent on her willing ravishment.

She felt his muscles go limp and he let out a soft snore. So cute. He'd fallen asleep.

Or passed out?

Oops. That. Matt had been in a Tsunami-for-Two haze and she'd let him sweep her into his bed. Stone-cold sober, she'd behaved like the party girl she'd sworn not to be.

While Matt snored softly beneath her, she lay alone with the hard reality that she'd slept with her *boss*. Despair swelled in her chest. The sexy sweat suddenly felt clammy, the sweet postcoital intimacy a guilty crime. She had to get away, escape from her mistake.

She slipped out of bed, careful not to wake Matt, who in his sleep made a patting gesture, as if to reassure her. He lay there, naked.

She sighed, covering him with the side of the bed-spread to prevent temptation, then tucking it under his chin so he wouldn't become chilled in the night.

Could he possibly be too drunk to remember this?

No way.

Now what? In a weak moment, she'd given in and

now there would be hell to pay. She put on her bikini and tiptoed out of the house, heading home. The playful moon seemed to taunt her. If she'd had a shoe, she'd have thrown it.

6

CANDY AWOKE TO THE SOUND of Sara whispering into the phone as she thumped down the stairs that ended a few yards from Candy's foldout bed.

"I faxed it, Uncle Spence," she said. "I'm telling you."

Candy squinted at the wall clock. Quarter to six. Uncle Spence was an early riser.

"No," Sara continued into the phone. "Yes… Like I said… Just check with Amy. I'm sure she has it." Reaching the bottom step, Sara caught sight of Candy and cringed in apology.

Candy mouthed, "It's okay."

Sara moved into the kitchen and began making coffee, the cell phone propped beneath her ear.

Candy flopped back onto the pillow, memories of last night flooding in like an early tide, gunky with seaweed. Would what happened in Malibu stay in Malibu?

Hardly. It would ride all the way to L.A. with them and up sixteen floors to the SyncUp office and ruin everything. Her and Matt's working relationship. Her chance for promotion. The tentative improvement in Matt's impression of her. Everything.

For a moment, she wanted to curl in a ball and burst

into tears. Instead she sat up. This was a mere setback. A pothole in her career path she would patch up and march over.

First, she'd go over to Matt's as she'd planned and act normal, treat last night like a drunken boo-boo. Never mind that she hadn't had a drop of liquor. They would laugh about it and move on. Proceed with Plan A.

She'd show Matt her work, do his makeover, teach him more about networking, then talk about the festival events she'd promised the girls she and Matt would do.

What other choice did she have?

Matt would probably be relieved. He'd be hungover and blaming himself, even though Candy knew it was her fault. Matt had been in unfamiliar territory—Drunk-and-Crazy Land, which was Candy's weekend hangout.

She made up the sofa, the sheets sticking out a bit, like her own doubts, then headed for the kitchen for coffee. En route, she paused to turn on Matt's computer.

She would get her notes together, call Freeda for her files, then head over to Matt's at 7:30, as agreed. Matt said he was up by 6:00, plus the hangover would wake him early. Soon, they'd be back on track—the sex a fading faux pas.

The sex. She sighed. She could still feel Matt inside her.

Sara handed her a mug of coffee. "Sorry I woke you."

"If you'd stop answering, Uncle Spence would stop calling."

"It's not that easy. He catches me just often enough to keep at it. I'm like a slot machine. What do they call that in behavior modification theory? A variable schedule of reinforcement?"

"This is your vacation."

"Look at *you,* already firing up the laptop." Sara nodded at where the computer shone at her, waiting. "You're scaring me, darlin'. Don't go to the dark side—all work and no play. That way lies madness."

"I have a plan, don't worry." Candy added cream and sweetener, then sipped the Kona coffee from Dark Gothic Roast that was Sara's favorite. Ellie had brought a freshly ground bag of their favorite flavor for each of them.

"I had a plan, too, and see where I am—getting wake-up calls from my uncle." Sara sighed, sipped her coffee, then looked at Candy. "So, you went out after your swim, right?"

"Right."

Sara leaned in, staring at Candy's neck. "Is that what I think it is?" Her eyes went wide. "It is. It's a hickey. What happened?"

"Shh." She put her finger to her lips. "Not a word to Ellie. Matt got drunk and we kind of made out."

"Made out? Uh-uh. You *slept* with him!" She half whispered, half squealed the words.

"It was a mistake. And I'm pretending it didn't happen. And you have to, too. Ellie will never let me hear the end of it."

"You are pure inspiration to me," Sara said, her low voice full of laughter.

"I shouldn't be. This is so…shortsighted. Irresponsible. Immature. Childish, really."

"Is this about your brothers again? Big brothers always baby their little sisters."

"It's not just that. My brothers were partners in

their firms by the time they were my age. I'm like a joke to them."

"We all get locked in our sibling positions. No matter what we accomplish. I'm sure the president has to call if he'll be late to dinner at his mom's."

"The point is that sleeping with Matt was the last thing I should have done in my situation." She shook her head, painfully pissed at herself.

"You'll recover. You are the most determined woman I know. You don't give yourself enough credit."

"Thanks for the support, Sara. Now allow me to help you." She held down the off button on Sara's cell. "Voice mail is your friend." She handed the dead phone over.

She grimaced. "I'm trying. Truly."

Candy glanced over at Sara's laptop. "Should I hide that thing so you can't work on it?"

"Not yet. I'm weaning myself. Really."

"Today, you're going to ask for surfing lessons, right? It's your duty to the team."

"We do need the points." Sara brightened, as if turning it into a duty meant she could safely do it.

"How about this? You try to enjoy yourself today, Sara, and I'll try not to."

Sara gave a rueful laugh, then glanced at the clock. "It's six. I need to roust Ellie for her audition. I'm doing her makeup. Wish me luck."

"How did her hair turn out?"

"I think gorgeous. She's not so sure."

"Change is not for wimps or sissies."

"Amen to that." Sara saluted her with her mug.

Candy showered and dressed, careful to mask her love bite with plenty of foundation. Twenty minutes later, she was working at the computer, while Ellie moaned about the audition and Sara chased her around the condo with an eye-shadow palette.

Freeda was at work when Candy called and easily sent her the files she needed. Candy double-checked her PowerPoint presentation, got everything in order and made a few notes. It took hardly any time, which made her feel better about blowing off work the evening before with Matt.

What she'd prepared would really show him why she'd make a great team leader. Candy could name three shoo-ins and a most-likely for four of the team leader spots. She had her heart set on the fifth one. She had the advantage of more marketing experience than anyone else Matt could possibly consider. Her secret weapons were fresh ideas, creativity and the dedication she was showing Matt this week.

Finished, she shut down the computer, put it in the bag, then mixed up a glass of her patented hangover cure to take to Matt. She was *good*.

She set off, the gently crisp air adding to her high spirits. Only a few surfers were in the water and a handful of people ran along the beach. Radar, her kindred spirit, was nowhere to be found. Maybe her work ethic had chased him away.

She knocked at Matt's door. No answer.

Could he still be asleep? Or was he in the shower? She went to the back of his place and peered in his bedroom window.

He was in bed, lying on his stomach. He'd kicked off most of the bedspread so that his bare ass and one leg were in full view. Her heart practically stopped at the sight.

His dark hair was dramatic against the white spread. His butt muscles dipped and swelled. She noticed a beauty mark high on the left cheek—the mate to the one on his face.

She was staring like a Peeping Tom, but it felt more like visiting a museum, studying a gorgeous statue: *Man at Rest.*

And she'd had him in action mere hours ago. The memory made her ache in delicate places.

She released a sigh and rested her forehead on the screen, making it rattle against the window.

Matt lifted his head at the sound, then pressed his temples, as if in pain. Sitting up, he saw her. His lips moved—saying her name, she'd bet. He tugged the spread around his waist and staggered to the window, which he opened. "Why did you leave?" He blinked at her through the screen, looking adorably sleepy.

"I was restless. And I had work to do."

He squinted at his watch, but that seemed to hurt, too. "It's only seven-thirty."

"Sorry I woke you, but you said you were up by six. Should I come back later?"

"No, no, it's fine," he said, trying to smile, but only managing a wince.

"Dr. Candy to the rescue." She lifted the glass. "My patented hangover cure."

"I'll meet you at the door." He turned and plodded away, the bedspread slipping deliciously low on his behind, so that his beauty mark seemed to wink at her. Mmm.

He let her in, then looked her over dreamily. "How are you, Candy?"

She fought the melting feeling and held out the glass. "Better than you, I bet."

"You look great," he said, his eyes roving her face, then her body, then back up to stop at her neck. "Did I do that?" He touched the hickey.

"I tried to cover it up," she said.

"Don't. It's cute." He looked almost proud.

"Here." She put the glass in his hand. "It's got OJ, an egg, protein powder and a dash of vodka. Wait, though. You need B vitamins." She put the computer down and fished out two capsules from the pillbox in her purse.

"Take these, drink it all down, then take a cool shower so your capillaries won't swell. That causes more pain. The final touch is a scalp massage."

"You're taking care of me." He grinned goofily.

"Trying to. Now drink."

Obediently, he took the vitamins and emptied the glass. "Not bad," he said, smacking his lips.

"Now the shower."

"How about you come with?" he asked, low and slow. His wrap hung low and she glanced down to see an unmistakable bulge.

She forced herself to stay on task. "I already showered."

"You can never be too clean." He reached for her.

She sidestepped. "Matt. We have to forget last night."

"Not possible."

"It has to be. You were drunk. I was…stupid. We work together."

"We're on vacation. What happens in Malibu, stays in Malibu?"

His argument was tempting, but no. "Last night was—"

"Great," he said.

"It was crazy," she corrected, fighting the urge to go with what he was saying, keep it up, stay in the fog of desire. "It was the time, the place, the booze. We were two warm bodies acting on natural urges. Under normal circumstances, we'd never be together, right? We're like apples and oranges, oil and water…."

"Gasoline and a match." His voice had a rough, sexy edge.

"Yeah. That." She felt herself weaken, watched his fingers at his waist, thought about how nimble they were. If he would just drop that bedspread, they could get down to business.

No. Control yourself. "Come on," she said as if he were being ridiculous. "The two of us? I mean, you're not my type." That sounded harsh and hurt flickered in his face, so she fixed it. "And I'm not yours, either. Right?"

"Right," he said stiffly, tightening his fist in the wadded sheet. "Of course. I'll get dressed." He turned to go, looking so defeated her heart ached.

Except in bed, she wanted to call after him. *In bed, you're more my type than anyone. Ever.* But this was best.

While he showered, she'd make him breakfast and fire up the computer. After that, they'd hit the mall for his makeover. She had a plan and she was sticking with it. Never mind that Matt was naked and wet and soapy…and did his shower have a pulsing nozzle?

While the computer booted, Candy made a pot of Columbian, Matt's favorite blend. Ellie had bought bagels, cream cheese and lox, so Candy toasted the bagels. The lox had omega-3, which would aid Matt's brain's recovery from the alcohol.

Back at the computer, she opened up her files, then located the Web site for the Malibu Country Mart and wrote down the numbers of the hair salon and optician. By the time Matt emerged, she was setting loaded plates beside two steaming mugs of fresh coffee.

"Better?" she asked him.

"A little, I guess." He looked pale and moved like a recovering accident victim.

"The food should help." She handed him his coffee, which he sipped tentatively. He looked so good in ordinary Dockers and a short-sleeved plaid shirt that she was ready to shove him against a wall and climb all over him.

Instead, she settled onto a stool beside him to watch him eat while nibbling on her own bagel.

"This is working," he said after a few bites. "Thanks."

It was working on her, too. Watching his mouth and fingers move as he ate, remembering where they'd been on her body, made her lose her appetite completely.

She went to wait for him at the computer.

He joined her, sitting on the chair she'd placed close to hers so they could both see the screen. When their thighs touched, she sucked in a breath so sharply she sounded like she'd been stabbed.

"You okay?" he asked, concerned.

"Of course. Sure." Her reaction embarrassed her.

"So, that last part…of the hangover cure?" He grinned.

Hell, she'd forgotten about the scalp massage. "Sure. Face this way."

He turned his chair and she scooted so that their legs were interlaced and they were mere inches apart, his breath, smelling of coffee and toothpaste, warm on her skin. She couldn't stare into his eyes—intense even through the glasses—so she told him to close his eyes. When he did, she slid her fingers into his wet hair and began to squeeze his scalp. "This will stimulate circulation and soothe the nerve endings. You'd be surprised how many there are in your scalp."

She worked her fingers slowly across his skull, starting at his crown, then working her way to his forehead. With his eyes closed, she was free to study his face, which was smooth and handsome and newly tanned from the volleyball game. That made the laugh lines beside his lips and the crinkles around his eyes more vivid.

"Man, that's good. It's like you released rubber bands from my skull."

"I'm glad you're enjoying it." She spied that beauty mark on his cheek and thought about the matching one on his behind. *Oh, Matt.* Now that she'd slept with him, the temptation was even stronger.

"You sure know your way around a hangover," Matt said.

That stung. "I'm hardly an expert. I talk to people. I've read tips."

Matt opened his eyes. "That was a compliment, Candy. I meant to say you are a knowledgeable person."

"If I were that good, I'd have insisted you drink less Tsunami and more club soda."

"I knew what I was doing, Candy." He grabbed her gaze. "Every minute."

"Oh." The heat in his words shot through her. "Close your eyes," she demanded.

He did and she focused on her task, moving to his neck to work her fingers along the cords of muscles, digging where muscle met ligament and ligament met bone.

Matt moaned the way he had last night and she went tight all over.

"That's enough of this," she said, patting his shoulder. It was all she could bear.

He opened his eyes and smiled. "Thanks. All that's left is the steel wool between my ears."

"That'll take more time."

"I'm never drinking again," he said, then held up his hands. "I know, I know. Everyone says that."

"Just stay clear of Tsunamis, huh?"

"Good advice."

"Shall we?" She indicated the computer screen before them, her anticipation helping her ignore Matt's nearness, his smell, the way the sun snagged in his hair and made it gleam.

"So what have you got for me?" Matt said, blinking against the brightness of the screen, poor thing.

In answer, she clicked the lead slide, *Ledger Lite Personal*, with the artwork she'd had a friend in graphics mock up for her. A second click revealed the tagline: *The powerful business solution now perfect for personal use.*

"The idea is to pare Ledger Lite to the basic ledger

and planning sheets, down-price it and market it for consumers and small business."

"Interesting," Matt said. "Small business, you say?"

"Yep. Like I told you, I've been talking to Gina in customer relations and she says people using Payroll Plus are asking for a simpler, cheaper version of LL."

"You have hard data to that effect?"

"Gina has a list of clients who'd happily test it and be our word-of-mouth network hubs."

"Who's already in the market?"

"We'll blow the competitors right out of the water, Matt. They're at higher price points, their programs are unwieldy, the menus counterintuitive. Nothing like the simplicity we've got built in with LL."

"The packaging you're showing is pricey."

"We could scale it back. This is just a mock-up."

"Our strategy is market expansion for Ledger Lite. A new niche would dilute that."

"But it's not new. That's what's cool. We're already a preferred provider with Payroll Plus. We have seventy-five percent penetration with small business. So, no need to buy lists or cold-market at all."

"You've got the numbers on that?"

"I was talking to Bud in R & D, yeah."

He nodded slowly. "This would require a new interface. Lots of code hours."

"Not if we adapted programming from a consumer product."

"It would be a scratch effort. And our programmers are swamped with the fall releases."

Candy's heart was pounding in her ears. He

seemed impressed, yet he shot down each answer with a new question.

"You seem skeptical. I can get more data, if that's all."

"That would help, because this would mean a big shift." He hesitated. "It's a good idea, Candy."

"What's missing?"

"The numbers, of course. It's something to consider." He smiled at her. *Nice try, kid.* She felt a mix of plunging disappointment and sharp fury. Why was he treating her this way?

"I have to ask…if Dave or Jim Daltry or Susan came to you with this idea, would you react differently?" Those three were definite team leaders.

"Of course not." He looked startled. "We'll consider it, like I said. Get the numbers for me and down the line we'll—"

"Ledger Lite goes into beta in two weeks. It can't be down the line. Can't we talk with the programmers, see if they can fit it in?"

He studied her. "Scott would have to decide that. I'd need something to pitch to him."

"A full marketing plan? No problem. I'll do that tomorrow."

"Candy, that's crazy. This is your vacation. It can wait."

"Not if we want to make beta."

"You're serious?"

"Of course." She watched as Matt gradually realized she'd meant what she'd said. It was hard not to wonder if he'd be as slow to accept the word of the key staff she'd mentioned.

"Get me a full marketing plan and we'll see."

"Great. Terrific." She had a chance. All she had to do was beef up her proposal. She'd work between festival events and nail it. Maybe it was better that he'd had questions and concerns. She'd prove she could accept criticism, modify her work, be resilient—all important management skills, all things that would make her a great team leader.

"So, are we done here?" Matt said, stifling a yawn. "Sorry. Caffeine's wearing off." He smiled, his eyes watery. The poor man was still hung over.

"For now, yeah." They'd gotten past the sex thing and were back to Plan A, so it was all good. "On to the mall now."

Matt groaned. "Can we get coffee there?"

"Absolutely."

In a half hour, they were strolling through the Malibu Country Mart, a friendly collection of boutiques boasting loads of greenery, flowers and arches, a rest area with a sandy playground and a view of the beach.

"I need a fill-up." Matt held the door to a Coffee Bean and Tea Leaf café for her.

"You're buying from one of Ellie's competitors?"

"People go to Dark Gothic Roast for Ellie as much as the coffee. No one can compete with that."

"True." She liked how well Matt knew his sister and how obvious his affection for her was.

At the oak counter, Candy studied the menu.

"I think you'll want the macchiato with an extra shot of espresso," Matt said. "It's the closest to café de Sade."

She jerked her gaze to his. "You know my coffee?"

"And you take it with sweetener, cream and cinnamon."

"Ah. You're remembering the time I sprinkled your shoes."

Another awkward Dark Gothic Roast meeting. She'd been relieved she hadn't added scalding coffee to the cinnamon topping she'd applied to Matt's wing tips.

"I just know what you like."

In bed. The message was clear. "Oh." Heat rose between them and she knew they were both remembering their erotic encounter.

"Can I help you?" the clerk asked.

"Uh, yeah," Matt said, jerked out of the moment. "She'll have the machiatto with a shot of espresso."

"And he'll have Columbian regular," Candy said. When the clerk left, she turned to him. "Black, right? I know what you like, too."

"Oh, yeah. You do." More heat, more trembling.

Somehow, they made it to a table, and she vowed to keep her mind on their professional relationship, not their recent intimacy.

"Nice job on the PowerPoint," Matt said, clearly trying to shift the topic. Did he sound surprised?

She realized she should clear up another misconception he probably had about her. "That reminds me, while we're overcoming bad impressions, I want to explain about that report I was late with—the next morning? After I fell?"

"The report that was missing pages and riddled with typos? I don't remember that one."

She cringed inside. "Exactly. You see what happened was—"

"It's water under the bridge. You don't have to explain."

"I *need* to explain. The reason I was late was I had to help my neighbor look for her lost dog. She was sobbing in the parking lot, so what could I do?"

"Express sympathy and get to work on time?" But he smiled, teasing her. "You could never do that." He leaned closer and she realized she'd moved in, too, her head at a flirty angle. They were behaving like lovers in public, hinting at secret moments they'd shared. Sex had changed their rapport, which wasn't good, no matter how lovely it felt.

She sat back and folded her arms across her chest. "Anyway, helping her made me late and I'd forgotten that I hadn't finalized the report. It was not like me. I meet deadlines and am committed to quality and—"

"Did you find the dog?"

"The dog? Oh. Yes. Covered in mud. You should have seen my backseat, but we found her."

"So it was worth it."

"Except that it left you with a bad taste in your mouth about me."

"I think you tasted quite nice that night. Sweet and salty from the margarita. Spicy, too. Your own taste."

His words set her entire body on fire. How was she supposed to talk about work when this could happen so easily?

"The point is that I'm responsible and dependable and—"

"Your work speaks for itself, Candy. If this is about me being your boss, I wish you'd forget it. You're fine with me. I know your strengths."

And her weaknesses? Would they keep him from

choosing her as a team leader? She was dying to ask, but that seemed inappropriate and too pushy.

The clerk called out their orders, then Candy took hers to the condiment station. When she returned to the table, Matt said, "I don't get why you ruin perfectly good coffee with all that junk." He nodded at her cup, which she was still stirring.

"Because plain coffee is boring. I like to change it up."

"Why change something that's already great?"

"To make it better?"

"I guess we see things differently," he said, which was a perfect reminder. They'd had a one-of-a-kind sexual head-on that would have never happened in the real world where their romantic interests were as different as their taste in coffee.

"So, on this makeover…" Matt said, obviously changing the subject. "You're not going for blue hair or anything, right?"

"Hmm. Not sure." She looked at him through a picture frame of her thumbs and index fingers. "Blue would clash with your eyes. Maybe magenta." She sipped more coffee.

"Lord. I'm putting myself in your hands, you know."

"Yeah. You said that."

Her fingers trembled, so she put down her cup. They both took shaky breaths. Matt seemed to force a smile.

"I'm glad we straightened things out," Candy said. "About the report and about that night."

"You see I'm not the complete dork I was that night?"

"I was the one with my thong on display."

"Ah, the thong…" He smiled wistfully. "I loved the

thong. Tiger-striped, too. Are those things as uncomfortable as they look?"

"You get used to it," she said, feeling herself blush.

"I speak for all men when I say thank you for making the effort." He tapped his cup against hers.

"So you enjoyed my humiliation?"

"Not the humiliation part. The thong part, yeah."

They both chuckled, the sound blending like music in the small shop, then fading, though they held each other's gaze.

"How's the hangover doing?" she asked.

"Better," he said, as if he'd forgotten. "You were right."

"I'm right a lot," she said.

"I have no doubt. I had fun yesterday, hangover notwithstanding." His eyes were soft and his smile spread. "I don't even regret the karaoke."

"Why would you? We were great together." She heard "You're the One that I Want" again in her head. "How about the dancing? Did you like that?"

"With you, sure."

"I mean the girl grinding on you."

"That was weird. I felt like a pole in a strip club."

"Surely it was nicer than that."

"It depends on who's doing the rubbing."

"I guess." Every time he made a remark like that she got a zing. It was wearing her out. She remembered she hadn't told him about the girls' plan for the festival competition.

"Listen, Matt, there's something I want to ask you."

"Definitely not magenta," he said.

"No. It's about the festival." She told him about the

competition, the prize, Sara's spreadsheet and the points he'd already helped them win.

"So I take it I'm your teammate?" he asked.

"I promised them we'd do some of the events, yes."

"Nothing too humiliating, I hope."

"Depends on how you feel about Jell-O wrestling."

"With you, I'd consider it." He winked, making her tremble like the gelatin dessert they were discussing.

"Red Jell-O stains, so forget that."

"Damn," he said, snapping his fingers in pretend dismay.

"But how about a limbo contest? It's early—before the Hot Shot Scavenger Hunt."

"Limbo? Backbends to music? Doesn't sound like me."

"Sure it does. It sounds exactly like Fun Guy. Plus it'll be networking practice."

Matt sighed. "You could talk me into anything, Candy. Like I said before, I'm in your hands."

And that was both delightful and scary. She could end up with the promotion she craved or in deep professional weeds, depending on how she handled herself.

7

THE NEXT THING MATT knew, Candy was hustling him past the shops toward his appointment with an optician, babbling about how contacts would let him see the world in a whole new way, and wouldn't that be fabulous?

For a moment, he longed to be back at the beach house quietly catching up on work, not jangled and tugged and hassled by his chirpy colleague. He'd almost ditched the hangover, but Candy made his head hurt all over again.

"While you're getting fitted for lenses, I'll pick out clothes you can try on. Multitasking. Sound good?"

"Sure." She was so damned eager to fix him up, he could hardly say no.

"Your hair appointment's in an hour. In between, we'll collect some business cards."

"Business cards?"

"Networking practice. We're competing for business cards, remember?"

"Uh, sure. I guess. Sounds…hectic." He was having enough trouble with losing his glasses and whatever hair style she would cook up. No dye. Or bleach. He'd say no to that.

"That's how I like to work, Matt. Efficient, organized, on top of things, never waste a minute." She snapped her fingers three times.

"Unless a neighbor's got a missing dog."

"That was an unusual case." She frowned at him.

"I'm joking, okay?" What was with her? She kept trying to hide her personality, pointing out how non-Candy she could be. It was as though she were interviewing for her job. That was a downside to becoming a manager. People stopped behaving normally around you. He hated that. In fact, he intended to talk about it at the first meeting of his new teams.

That made his gut clutch. He should be planning the teams now instead of dawdling at a mall. He had to consider skills, knowledge, work style, potential and, thanks to the PQ2, personality. Everyone had pros and cons and some people worked better with others.

Candy was one of his problem placements. She was creative and a high producer, typo-laden report notwithstanding. He wished he could clone her for all five teams.

He'd love to set her up to float, but that wouldn't work. To ensure mutual responsibility, the teams had to be self-sufficient. Only outside consultants worked that way. If only Candy were one. She'd perform rings around the guy Scott hired when they were overloaded or stumped.

Matt had to figure out where to put her. And where everyone else would work best. The personnel aspects of the VP job were his weak point. It was related to his lack of people skills, he guessed. What had Candy said he was? Nonsocial. Yeah. He smiled.

Hell, Candy could put the teams together in a heart-beat. She knew everyone down to shoe sizes. He'd love to get her opinion, but that was impossible. Inappropriate with someone he supervised.

Even worse now that they'd slept together. Candy had had to shake him from his sexual haze, reminding him that a perfect storm of booze, vacation and opportunity had brought them together.

You're not my type. She'd had to remind him. She was right, but it hurt to hear. He should be grateful she'd been so eager to forget what had happened. For all her wild ways, she was a practical person. He still felt uneasy, though. What he'd done was so out of character, even taking the Tsunami into account, he hardly recognized himself. After Candy was finished with him today, he'd *look* like a stranger, too.

At the eyeglass place, Candy signed him in and breezed off to select a new wardrobe, intent on her role as his female Henry Higgins, transforming him into Fun Guy.

When Candy returned, the optician was watching him practice putting the blasted lenses into his eyes. He'd flipped the right lens across the room, then onto his shoe. The left one was now tucked so far back under his eyelid it might require surgery to remove. No way would he go through this hassle every morning.

"Let me see how you look," Candy said.

"Hang on." He dug deep enough to bruise his eyeball, captured the plastic disk and centered it over his pupil. He blinked and Candy's face swam into focus, almost making it worth the trouble.

"Oh, you look great," Candy breathed. "Doesn't he?"

"He has nice eyes," the optician—Carol—said. "Very blue. They remind me of Greg Kinnear's."

"Exactly," Candy said. "Or maybe Patrick Dempsey's?"

"Oooh," she said. "From *Grey's Anatomy?* Him, too."

"Thanks, I guess." Matt cleared his throat, embarrassed to have two women carrying on about his eyes.

A clerk bagged up his paraphernalia—cases, cleaning fluids, spare lenses—and rang up the charges and he had to blink repeatedly to see clearly enough to determine whether he had a credit card or his driver's license in his hand.

Once outside the shop, Candy danced backward in front of him as they walked. "Isn't it great to be free of glasses?"

He blinked and squinted, fighting the lenses, which slid across his eyes like a car on ice. "I guess."

"It feels funny at first, I know. That's why you're blinking so much. Soon you'll be used to them."

"I hope so."

"It's so worth it. No dents on your nose. Full peripheral vision. No steamed-up glasses when you make pasta. You can see to swim and in the shower and in bed at night. No bumping glasses when you kiss." She stopped abruptly. "I mean… Anyway…I can really see your eyes now," she said.

"So you feel closer to me?"

"Matt," she said, warning him away from that kind of talk. He liked the way color flared in her cheeks, visible even under the pink from yesterday's sun.

"We've got thirty minutes before your haircut, so let's go for some business cards."

They agreed to meet at the hair salon and he watched her walk away, sandals clacking, butt tight, hips rocking in that irresistible way she had…. Damn.

Thirty minutes and six business cards later, Matt entered the hair salon, which smelled so strongly of hairspray his eyes watered. Personally, he preferred an old-fashioned barber shop.

He was relieved to see he wasn't the only male customer in the place. One guy was in a recliner at the sinks getting his hair washed and another was getting aluminum-foil squares painted into his hair. What? No way would he allow that to be done to him.

Candy waved him over, grinning and eager, and he realized he'd get cornrows and a lip piercing if she wanted it. What a chump he was.

"Here he is, Raul," Candy said, when he reached her. "Raul, this is Matt. Matt, this is Raul and we are so lucky he could squeeze us in."

"Sit." Raul patted the back of the chair. "Let's see what I have to work with." Once Matt was in place, Raul ran his fingers through Matt's hair, then fiddled with the ends, making shocked noises. "Look at that… So damaged… You're using a harsh shampoo… And no conditioner. Men!"

He blew out a breath, then spoke to Candy. "Why they think it's macho to neglect their hair, I'll never understand."

He braced his fingertips at the top of Matt's head and wiggled them around, frowning like a doctor with a dif-

ficult diagnosis. "Light curl…lots of body…thick…"
He fingered a strand, then dropped it, a scientist evalu-
ating an experiment.

"Is that good?" Matt ventured.

Raul jerked his eyes to the mirror, as if startled that
his victim was alive. "For some things." He put his finger
to his chin and stared at Matt's reflection. "I'm thinking
texturing, short in the back, tapered for style. Razor the
ends. Oh, and a definite weave. Golden ash, I think."

"A weave?" Matt said. Was that like braids?

Raul flipped open a notebook that held tiny whisk
brooms of hair in a million shades. He held one next to
Matt's face. "Maybe honey blond?" He seemed to be
talking to Candy now. "It'll bring out his eyes. He has
the best eyes. Brad Pitt without the smoky green."

"The optician said Greg Kinnear," Candy said. "But
I was thinking Patrick Dempsey."

"Not quite. Keifer Sutherland maybe? Anyway,
gorgeous. So, honey blond it is." He whipped away the
hair and shut the notebook.

"Hold it," Matt said, figuring out where this was
going. "You're not dying my hair blond."

"It's just highlights, Matt," Candy said. "Your hair will
look sun-kissed. That's how they do it." She pointed at
the foiled-up guy who was now under a dryer. A dryer?

"No. No way. Just a cut. You can do the razor thing,
but no sun-kissing anything."

Raul and Candy looked at each other.

"I think he means it," Candy said with a sigh.

"Shame." Raul shook his head, acting like a surgeon
forced to settle for a bypass, when he'd wanted a full

transplant, but he went after Matt with several kinds of scissors and some electric clippers, talking with Candy about movies and celebrity adoptions the whole time. They acted as if they'd known each other for years instead of minutes. That was Candy all the way.

One good thing about the contact lenses was that he could see her clearly in the mirror. He'd always had to remove his glasses for haircuts. She sat on the stool to his right, skirt riding high, swinging her leg, her sandal heel dangling.

He found himself lulled by Raul's snips and tugs and the music of Candy's voice, her light laughter, her chatter. After the cutting, Raul rubbed in some gel, then some foam, then a spray and finally pointed Matt's chair at the mirror. "There," he said. "Is it magic or is it magic?"

It wasn't too bad. Short on the sides and back, the longer top part stuck up a little from the goo, which made it too shiny for his taste, but he could live with the cut. Matt was relieved. It could have been so much worse.

"It's magic, Raul," Candy said, answering for him. "Isn't it?" she asked the woman in the next chair.

"Gorgeous," the woman said. "Especially with his eyes. I think definitely Greg Kinnear."

"Maybe you're right," Candy said, tilting her head to study him more closely.

Mortified, he cleared his throat. "What's the maintenance on this?" He'd sounded like he was discussing an oil change.

"Sculpting wax and a bit of root lift. Ten minutes maybe?"

"Wax? Root lift?"

Raul sighed. "Oh, be that way." He scrubbed Matt's hair the way Matt usually did when he got out of the shower. "You can do that if you want to waste my work."

"Great." He released a breath, but at the counter he let Raul convince him to buy some wax just in case. One hefty check later, he let Candy lead him to a menswear boutique.

The saleswoman, whom Candy knew by name, took them to a booth beside a rack loaded with clothes that he was dismayed to learn were all for him. Something about mixing and matching…

The saleswoman and Candy fluttered around him as he put on and took off suits, blazers, pants, dress shirts, summer shirts, shorts and swim trunks until his skin felt raw.

Candy was a whirl of energy and opinion. Yes to this, no to this, maybe on this, her features screwed up as she analyzed each item for fit, color and style.

Whenever he stepped out of the changing booth, Candy ran her fingers along the shoulder seams, messed with his sleeves and cuffs, checked the break at the tops of his shoes. Her busy fingers were on him everywhere, making him sweat, making him think about last night. Needless to say, he wrote a lot of code in his head to keep from stacking wood.

After a wearying hour of this, he'd just stripped down to his boxers, when Candy spun into the booth. "One more—oh! Sorry. You're almost—" Her eyes darted to his boxers, which, of course, bulged.

"Oh." Her eyes zoomed to his, heat sizzling there. "Do you need…underwear? They have some nice silk boxers…out…there." She waved aimlessly behind her.

"I'm equipped," he said.

"Oh, yeah," she said. "Fully."

"I'm worn out with all this," he said, weary of the scrape of fabric, the constant struggle to control himself around her, to keep his arms from holding her, his mouth from taking hers.

"Oh, me, too," she said, her shoulders sagging. "You've got a good start anyway. Maybe wear the Hawaiian shirt and board shorts out?"

"Okay," he said. He changed into the items she suggested.

When he stepped out of the dressing room, her eyes lit up and she gave a delighted gasp. "You look great. Come and see." She led him to the three-way mirror.

Not bad, he realized, studying his reflection. He still recognized himself, but he looked…sharper.

"Matt, version 2.0," she said.

He smiled, glad it wasn't so bad. He could have looked gay or vain or foolish, but he looked…decent. He'd been right to trust her.

"You're going to need non-prescription sunglasses," she said. "Hang on." She went to the rack by the register and came back with a pair she slid onto his nose, her fingers gentle at his temples, then stepped back to survey the effect.

"Wow," she breathed. "Women will go nuts for you and I'm not kidding."

How about you? Are you nuts for me? He couldn't help wanting to know that, could he?

"Not that you weren't attractive before, but now you're…enhanced." Her eyes roved over him, holding him so intently he felt like her fingers had actually touched him.

"Thanks, Candy. For doing this."

"My pleasure."

The last thing he wanted to think about at the moment was her pleasure. He knew exactly how she sounded, what she looked like, the way she stilled, then cried out.

Ouch.

"Are you hungry?" she asked softly.

"Starving," he answered, but neither of them seemed to be talking about food.

8

YOU SET YOURSELF UP, girl, Candy realized as they drove back from the mall, heading for the deli to appease their *hunger.* Like a couple of sandwiches from the chichi deli could relieve the ache inside her, the way she craved Matt's touch.

He'd been tough to resist before, but after the makeover, now that he *looked* like Fun Guy, he'd become one of those perfect sundaes where you licked the bowl afterward, with no regrets at all about blowing your diet because it was *so* worth it.

Now, she was depending on her weakest part—self control—to keep the lid on her feelings for the man.

All that time touching him while he tried on clothes had left her feeling raw and exposed, vulnerable to any glance or movement. When he tapped his finger on the steering wheel, she got a charge.

They would eat their sandwiches on the beach before the festival events began. That had been her stupid idea. It had sounded good at the time, but now she realized it meant more hours together non-stop. After they ate, it would be time for the limbo contest and then the photo hunt. The prospect exhausted her.

She racked her brain for some aspect of Matt that turned her off, some nerdy flaw, but she couldn't think of a single one. At the moment, Matt was a total hottie.

It's just the makeover effect, she told herself. *Merely a superficial change.* Matt was still the same distant, work-obsessed intellectual he'd been yesterday, locked in his head, glued to his keyboard. Hell, the man had to be forced to go on vacation. She'd had to drag him outside to notice the beauty of the beach, the sea, the moment. She did not relate at all.

She sighed and stared out the window.

Matt seemed lost in thought, too, staring ahead as he drove. The silence felt thick, but she didn't know if it was from sexual tension or mutual weariness, or both. She wasn't sure what Matt was feeling. When he'd said he'd had enough in the boutique, she'd thought it was because of all the touching they'd done, the close looks, the intimacy of seeing him nearly nude again. But maybe he'd just been sick of changing clothes. Worse, she didn't know which she wanted it to be.

At least the scenery was distracting. The ocean gleamed in the gathering sunset. It would be nice to watch the waves as they ate. She should appreciate whatever beach time she could net from this complicated vacation.

At the deli, while Matt picked out a bottle of wine, she visited with the clerk about the sandwich selections, finally settling on Black Forest ham with Dofino cheese on herbed focaccia fresh from the oven. The clerk seemed flattered by all her questions and offered the special honey-horseradish mustard sauce the employees usually kept for themselves, which she thought was sweet of him.

When Matt got out his wallet to pay, a couple of business cards fell to the floor. Candy picked them up. "Did you score these from the mall?"

"Yeah. I only got six though." He shrugged.

"That's excellent. Really."

"What about you?"

"I got twelve, but I got lucky. I ran into a bunch of sales guys at the juice bar. They live to hand out cards."

"Candy, if they'd been monks sworn to silence, you'd have them reciting poetry to you. Writing it on the spot."

She smiled, warmed by his compliment. "Anyway, with my handicap, that puts us neck-and-neck."

"Speaking of neck..." He brushed hers with his finger-tips. "It's showing." He meant the love bite he'd given her.

She shivered, thinking of how she'd gotten it, and put her finger there. It felt warm to the touch. "I'll use more makeup next time."

"Don't. I like seeing it. It reminds me...."

"Me, too," she said, her heart lifting at his words. Which was not helpful at all. It would be so much better if he showed more regret. If they both did. If they could forget it altogether. Paying up, they then drove to the beach house.

Before long, they found a great spot from which to watch the receding tide and settled on a rock outcropping to unpack their meal and pour wine into plastic goblets.

The lowering sun was painting the sky orange and pink, the ocean silver and bronze. A handful of surfers skimmed the sunset waves. It was a gift to be here, to enjoy this easy beauty. Candy breathed deeply of the sea air, letting it dissolve her tension, her aching desire for Matt.

"Isn't this a miracle?" she said. "Being here?"

"It is," he said, smiling warmly.

He made her feel…watched over. Protected. She'd never felt this way with a guy. Because she'd never settled on one? Or had she never chosen guys who gave off this vibe? She realized she liked it—this sense of connection, the security of being a couple.

It was completely false, though, to feel this way, however fleetingly, with Matt. They were actors in front of a blue screen on which exotic scenery had been projected. She was here because of work—they both were. This wasn't a romance and she didn't dare forget it.

She took a bite of her sandwich to distract herself. "Mmm, good sandwiches, huh?" She loved the combination of herb-infused bread, smoky sweet ham and creamy cheese. The dressing brought it all together with a little zing.

"Great choice, Candy. I would have just said two Number Ones and been content. You had the guy dragging out the best ham and the secret sauce."

"The sauce is great, huh? It blends the flavors and adds a surprise." Exactly how their sex had been—a blending and a surprise. *Stop that.*

She forced herself to make a point. "This is a good lesson, really. People love to share what they know, what they have—their secret sauce, really—if you show you're interested."

"Yeah, but you have a gift, Candy."

"What about you? You got six cards in a half hour."

"The sixth was a cheat. I asked a guy for directions to the salon and his cards were on a display rack at his elbow."

Candy laughed. "But you asked for directions! That's so brave. Men never ask for directions."

"Good point. Maybe this makeover is turning me into a girlie man." His eyes danced with mischief.

"No chance of that," she said softly, then quickly changed the subject. "So what worked with the business cards?"

"What you said about listening more than talking, I guess. I didn't feel like I had to entertain anyone. I met a couple of interesting people—one guy owns a worm farm and another builds bomb-safe doors for nuclear plants."

"How fascinating."

"Neither one needed software, so I don't know that I accomplished anything."

"So what? Side trips are the best part of life."

"Spoken like a person willing to blow an important meeting to chase a dog."

"I explained what happened, Matt," she said, stung by the zinger, just as she'd been when he'd called her an expert with hangovers and wild bar parties. Matt still didn't respect her enough. "It was a unique circumstance and—"

"Hey, that was a joke. I'm just getting the hang of Fun Guy and you're turning into Serious Girl on me?" He touched her cheek, coaxing her into a smile.

"Sorry. I'm…I guess I'm tired." She knew she couldn't demand Matt's respect; she had to earn it, but she still felt discouraged.

"Tell you what," Matt said, "here's what I want if I win our competition—come with me to the conference. Be my secret networking weapon. How's that?"

He was appeasing her, she knew, easing her hurt feelings, but she decided to make the most of it. "I'd be happy to go, whether you win or not. For you and SyncUp, I'm there." She ticked her plastic wine glass against his, then lifted it for a drink.

"Deal," he said.

"Great choice in wine, by the way."

"It was the best value at that price point."

"God, Matt. Couldn't you pretend you chose it for its smoky blackberry nose and clean finish?"

"Sorry." He winced in pretend regret.

"Have you always been that way? Cut to the chase, travel in straight lines, no chitchat, get the best value?"

"I guess so. Maybe it was because my mom depended on me after our dad left."

"That makes sense. Ellie told me a little about what happened." Ellie and Matt's mother came to L.A. to become an actress, but never quite made it. Flamboyant and emotionally fragile, she was wrecked when her husband left her.

"Ellie was young—six? How old were you?"

"Ten," Matt said.

"That must have been hard."

"Not so bad really. You do what you have to do when you're in the middle of things. Looking back, it seems sad, but at the time I liked the responsibility. I was proud my family could count on me. I liked being dependable. Then and now."

"But what about what you want? What feeds your soul?"

"Excuse me?" He shot her a questioning look. "You going woo-woo on me here?"

"It's an important question—whether you do what you do out of obligation or joy—don't you think?"

"You've had too much of this." He pretended to take her wine away. "Why can't it be both? I get satisfaction from my work. And I'm glad people count on me. It's who I am."

"Sure, but if your family situation had been different? If you hadn't been forced to grow up so fast, maybe you wouldn't have ended up so serious and focused."

"You say that like it's a bad thing." He smiled. "To you it is, I guess. I take it you had a carefree childhood?"

"Oh, yeah," she said. "I'm the youngest and I have two older brothers. Robert, the younger, is ten years older than me and Philip, twelve."

"So you were the baby? I bet they spoiled you."

"Of course." Her mouth twisted with that admission. "Maybe that's why it took me so long to get my act together in college."

"What do you mean?"

"I changed my major a bunch. First, I wanted to be a psychologist, then I studied art history, then creative writing, then I quit and worked for a while—for a direct-mail marketing firm, then an ad agency. I really liked advertising, so I finished up with a marketing degree. Finally."

"You figured it out." He was being kind.

"At twenty-four? Come on. Plus, after that I floated

freelance for a while, switched jobs a bunch. My brothers just shake their heads. They were partners in their law firms by the time they were my age. Philip's in corporate law and Robert's a litigator."

"Lots of people get degrees and still don't know what they want," Matt said. "And twenty-four is young."

"But I wasted time and money. My parents' money."

"Was it a sacrifice for them?"

"You mean financially? Not really, I guess. They're in good shape with money. They built their signage company from nothing to a factory with fifty employees. See? High achievers all around. Except for me. I'm the misfit."

"I'm sure they don't see you that way."

"They don't get me at all." She shook her head, weary of that status, then smiled at him. "Our childhoods were so different. Which do you think was better?" she mused. "Being too indulged or too burdened?"

"It's more a matter of fit, really, I think. If the way you're wired and the environment you grow up in match, things go smoothly. If not, there's friction."

She stared at him. She'd never thought about it that way before. "So my problem is I got the wrong family?"

He laughed. "I doubt it's ever that simple. In my case, the fit turned out to be right. I'm wired to be responsible and that's what my family needed. Of course Ellie took over supporting our mother after I went to college. She's wired that way, too."

He looked out across the ocean, swinging his plastic cup from his fingertips, the movement mesmerizing.

"Did you always know what you wanted to be when

you grew up?" she asked. "Were you born with a punch card in your fist?"

"Pretty much." He gave a soundless laugh. "I built my first computer from components at fourteen. That made computer engineering an obvious major."

"So how'd you get to SyncUp?"

"It fit my career path. I've chosen each job to broaden my experience and get more responsibility. I jumped at the spot at SyncUp. It's a great company and a tremendous opportunity. Scott's got vision."

"Yeah. I like Scott."

"What about SyncUp? Do you like working there?" He seemed to dig at her when he asked that, as if he expected her to say no.

"Of course. Why do you ask?"

"You stir up so much mischief, I thought you might be bored."

Bored? The word gave her a skittering feeling, as though the bottom had dropped from her stomach. Sure, her mind wandered during meetings and follow-up details irritated her. Once she'd figured something out, she wanted to move on. But did it show as boredom? Really? Is that what Matt thought?

She had to turn that around, make it show her aptitude for a promotion. "I like a challenge, Matt," she said. "I believe in meeting expectations and going the extra mile. Take stretch goals, for example. I believe in them. If you want to grow, you have to reach out of your comfort zone."

He held up his hand. "Whoa. This is starting to sound like a performance review. I'm asking as a friend, not as your boss."

"Oh. Sure. As a friend." Or a lover? They'd been lovers, after all. Which gave her a delicious thrill. It was so wild, so amazing. She'd slept with Matt Rockwell. It was hard to believe and, in a secret part of herself, she celebrated it.

The rest of her knew it was a mistake she had to forget.

As dusk gathered around them, though, she became more aware of details about Matt—the way he breathed and moved, the way his tan deepened as the light faded. He picked up a piece of driftwood and flung it into the sunset-silvered water and she liked the tensing of his muscles, his follow-through and the way he watched for the stick to land, then smiled.

Dusk seemed like a curtain drawing around them, making her want to tuck into the cave of his body, tip up her chin for a kiss. Let the darkening sky blanket them, cozy and intimate, after a long day spent in each other's company.

She realized she rarely spent entire *days* with a guy. They did movies, clubs, maybe a hike up Squaw Peak or a long mountain-bike ride. Sex, of course, sometimes with breakfast the next morning. But never more than a few hours at a time.

For hanging out, she preferred her friends—Ellie and Sara, when she could pry them away from work, and a couple of girlfriends from college. But she could see now that a steady guy, a regular relationship, had its rewards.

"You know, I've hardly thought of work at all," Matt said, his tone as wistful as her thoughts.

"That's good, isn't it? It's your vacation, after all."

"I suppose. I do have a crucial project next week that I should spend some time on while I'm here."

"Really? Can I help?"

His eyes shuttered away from her. "It's management stuff."

It was probably the teams. "I'd be happy to be a sounding board. I'm a good listener."

"Thanks, but I'd better handle it on my own."

"Do you like being a manager?" she asked.

"Yeah," he said, nodding thoughtfully. "Well, I did until the PQ2 came along." He laughed, then sipped his wine. "The people stuff intimidates me, but I'll figure it out."

"I'm sure you will."

"You're helping me with that," he said, looking at her.

"I'm glad." She held his gaze. *And you can help me,* she thought. *Make me a team leader.* It would be so easy to say it here at the shore, buzzed from wine, enjoying each other's company, sharing their histories, peeking at each other's inner selves. Matt liked her, would want to help her. Why not just come right out with it?

She opened her mouth to do it, except Matt's expression suddenly turned earnest. "Candy, listen, I need to apologize again for doing what I did last night. It was very irresponsible of me to act on an attraction—no matter how strong—to a colleague, especially someone I supervise."

His paternal tone irked her. As if he were the adult and she were the child. "I was there, too, remember? It takes two."

"But the burden is greater for me because of my status."

"What? Are you talking about sexual harassment? Please. Like I said, I was there, too."

"And you behaved very professionally this morning, suggesting we forget what happened. Thank you."

At least he'd given her that much credit.

"If what I did changed our work relationship—led to favoritism on my part or resentment on yours—I couldn't live with myself."

"Don't worry. It hasn't changed anything," she said. Except she felt an icy chill. She'd been ready to ask for the promotion, leaning on their new intimacy. What had she been thinking? She wanted the job on her own merits, not because Matt was hot for her or owed her a favor.

This was bad. Or maybe it was a natural mistake. She didn't know. She felt as if they'd thrown *personal* and *professional* into a blender and hit *pulverize.*

She was confused and disoriented, as if they'd crossed an irreversible line, changed their relationship forever.

She could not allow that. They had to move on, change the subject, get past this awkwardness.

"So, what's the proper attire for limbo?" Matt said, giving her a wry grin. He obviously wanted to change the subject, too.

"Good question. I need to change bikinis for something with more give."

"More give?" He swallowed hard, looking at her body, then away.

"Absolutely. And you should take off your shirt so it won't snag on the bar."

"I can't believe you talked me into this," Matt said, standing to remove his shirt.

She couldn't help staring at him, bare-chested and newly tanned. She wished she'd noticed more about his body when they'd been in bed together.

"Candy?"

She realized she was staring. "You're looking good," she said, pretending to evaluate him. "Your tan's nicely even." She ran her fingers along the faint sleeve line, raising goose bumps on his skin.

"Feels good," he rasped.

She lifted her finger, trying to ignore the simmering heat in his eyes, fighting her own reaction. "Do you feel more social?" she stammered. "More relaxed?"

"Do I seem that way to you?"

"Definitely."

"I don't feel that relaxed. And the longer we stand here, the worse it gets." His gaze settled on her mouth. He wanted to kiss her, she could tell, and, worse, she wanted him to. He dragged his eyes up to meet hers.

"Say something quick," he said, clearly wanting her to distract him.

"Time to limbo?" she said weakly.

He shook his head, as if that wasn't a good enough distraction.

She stepped back. "The point is, you look like Fun Guy. Scott will so approve of Fun Guy."

"Yeah?" He stepped closer.

"And Jane!" she blurted, realizing that was the way to go. "Jane will love Fun Guy."

"Jane?" He looked puzzled for a second. "She'd be surprised, for sure."

"So ask her out when you get back."

"There's no point to that."

"She broke up with you because you weren't any fun, but now you are. She'll give you another chance, I'm sure."

"What if I don't want that?"

"Sure you do. Talk to her. You gave up too soon."

He didn't say anything, just held her gaze. He had too much pride, probably, to admit he wanted Jane back.

Whatever. The idea that Matt was taken felt like a life raft to her. She never messed with taken guys.

Of course it was ridiculous that she needed more of a reason to stay clear than that Matt was her boss and sleeping with him might kill her promotion, but a little insurance never hurt, right?

IT WAS A LIE, MATT knew—not telling Candy he no longer wanted to be with Jane. But it could solve his problem.

He'd no sooner apologized to Candy for the sex, babbling on about his higher duty as a manager, than he'd been ready to haul her back to his place for more, like some randy caveman.

What the hell was wrong with him? He'd never read the SyncUp policy on fraternization, but he knew for certain that a manager sleeping with someone he supervised was a bad idea.

Moreover, Matt needed everyone's respect while he was organizing his department and he certainly didn't want to give Scott a reason to doubt his choice of Matt for VP.

Whatever it took to keep clear of her: If the idea of Jane made Candy step back, then he had a shred of hope he could control himself. No decent guy went after a new woman when he wanted to reconcile with his ex, right?

Around Candy, he felt pretty damn indecent. Now he

was walking her to her beach house for a bikini with more *give*. He hoped to hell that didn't mean more bare skin.

Too late, he realized his sister was likely to be inside. Ellie would definitely pick up the energy between them.

In self-defense, he put his shirt back on, just as Candy opened the door to music and the roar of a blender. Ellie was in the kitchen making drinks, while another woman hunched over a laptop, a cell phone at her ear. She waved at them, talking into the phone.

"Hey, guys," Ellie called from the kitchen, then bent down to peer at them from beneath the cabinets. "Omigod!" She hurried out to stare at him, hands to her cheeks in pretend shock. "What happened to you?"

Ellie herself had gone through some kind of transformation. She'd changed her hair and makeup so that she looked softer, more like the Ellie she'd been before she got into her Queen of the Damned phase.

"What have you done with my brother, Candy?" she demanded.

"Meet Fun Guy," Candy said with a sweep of her arm.

Ellie walked all around him. "I can't believe how different you look! No glasses. New hair. New clothes."

"Thanks," Matt said. "I like your new look, too."

She grabbed her hair self-consciously. "It was for the audition. It feels…funny."

"It looks great," Candy added.

"How did you get Matt to do this? I've been nagging him to lose the glasses for *years*. What did you say? What did you do? Never mind. Too personal. I don't want to know."

"Oh, stop," Matt said. "She updated my look so

Scott will see me as more, I don't know, social? Hip?" He shrugged.

"Whatever," Ellie said. "I've never seen you in a shirt this loud." She gave Candy a salaam. "I bow before you, O Queen of Makeovers."

"It's nothing," Candy said.

"Oh, yes it is. Doesn't he look great, Sara?" Ellie asked. "I'm going to get us all something to toast with." She headed for the kitchen.

"You look very nice, Matt." The woman had put down her phone and joined them. She smiled, telling him she knew how over-the-top Ellie could be. "I'm Sara."

"Pleased to meet you," Matt said, shaking Sara's hand. "I believe I've seen you at the coffee shop?"

She nodded.

"With a phone glued to her ear," Candy said. "Sara's always working."

"I'm with Anderson Title. On the tenth floor."

"Except on this trip she's *supposed* to be relaxing."

"Now stop right there," Sara said. "Not only did I sign up for the surfing competition, I asked Drew for lessons."

"You didn't! You did? Oh, that's great." Candy lunged forward to hug her friend, who did look a bit buttoned-down to be a surfer.

"And you and Drew…?" Candy asked breathlessly.

"Let's just say we'll be doing the photo scavenger hunt together." Sara went pink and Matt wanted to escape. He hadn't been trapped in a girl-talk session since Ellie was in high school.

"This is great," Candy said. "Isn't this great, Ellie?"

"That's why we're celebrating."

Ellie handed a margarita to Sara, then extended one to Candy, who shook her head. "We need our wits about us to do well in the limbo contest."

Plus, he needed every inhibition he could muster to override his attraction to Candy. He'd already seen the effect alcohol had on him.

"We're also celebrating because Ellie got the part!" Sara said. "She's an extra on *Sin on the Beach*."

"That's fabulous!" Candy hugged Ellie.

"Plus," Sara said, leaning in, "she connected with Bill Romero again and they're getting together tonight. For the scavenger hunt…and later."

Matt's ears perked. "Bill Romero? Is that the guy who used to live next door? The one you spied on all the time?"

Ellie slugged his arm. "I was only twelve and I was smitten. Now I can actually get words out." She abruptly looked twelve again, with a light in her eyes he'd never seen when she spoke about a guy. He felt a surge of happiness and hope. Maybe Ellie would let this guy in, allow someone to take care of her for a change. With all his heart, he hoped for her happiness.

"So, we've all got partners for the festival contests," Candy said. "Now we've got a serious chance to win."

So they were partners, huh? He wondered if Candy would tell her friends what had really happened between them. Before he'd gotten to know her, he'd have been positive she'd dish every detail, but now he'd seen her quiet, thoughtful side.

The more time he spent with her, the more he liked her. Which wasn't particularly helpful.

"Let me show y'all where we stand on the competition," Sara said, returning to her laptop. "With Ellie on the TV show and with what Candy and Matt earned already, we've got a good start. Ellie came up with a name for us. Team Java Mamas. Isn't it perfect? Considering Dark Gothic Roast and all."

"I love it," Candy said. They all looked over Sara's shoulder at the screen, where she clicked into a spreadsheet listing events, potential points and points earned.

"You're serious about this," Matt said, trying not to bury his nose in Candy's hair.

"Oh, Sara's serious about everything," Ellie said.

"You all will enjoy this when we win, so no bitching," Sara said. "Assuming we do well enough to make the finals, we'll need a killer essay."

"And Candy's our ace in the hole on that," Ellie said. "Isn't Candy amazing, Matt?" Ellie dug in with her gaze. "Do you know how lucky you are to have her?" She paused. "At SyncUp, I mean."

"I do. Yes." He glanced at her.

"I'm just part of the team," Candy said, flushing. Her vulnerability touched him. For someone so socially confident, she was surprisingly insecure about her work. He wanted to help her with that if he could, without getting too personal.

"What about the freak-dancing contest?" Ellie asked, pointing at the screen. "Matt, what do you think?"

"No way." He stepped back, hands up in protest.

"Come on. What did Candy call you? Fun Guy? Fun Guy would love it. I mean, you're doing the limbo? I wouldn't have believed anyone could talk you into that." She gave Candy a knowing look.

"I have to draw the line somewhere," he said, but Ellie had a point. Only Candy could have convinced him to sing karaoke, get contacts, do backbends in swim trunks—and whatever other goofy thing she had yet to talk him into.

Candy went off to change, leaving him with Ellie and Sara, who lapsed into a discussion of Ellie's new look, talking about bronzers and foundations and primer coats until he felt like they were debating building construction instead of cosmetics.

"What do you think, Matt? Should I keep up this illusion, this pretense, this false me?" Ellie asked him.

"You're asking a guy who just had a makeover," he said, then got serious. "You have to be comfortable with yourself, El. You have to like how you—"

Candy appeared, stopping him cold. She wore a white bikini held together by loose strings here and there.

"Yeah, Matt?" Ellie prompted. "I have to like how I…what?"

"How you look," he finished faintly, unable to take his eyes off Candy, who looked like an edible angel. A couple of tugs with his teeth and she'd be bare.

"Wow," he said, his voice a rasp over a suddenly dry throat. "That looks, um, like it has more give." He frowned, as if that were a serious consideration.

"More give?" Ellie asked.

"For better bending," Candy said.

Bending? God. "We'd better get moving," he said, hustling her toward the door before they endured more harassment.

"Have fun, you two," Ellie said. "How *low* can you go?"

He didn't want to think about it.

9

THE FESTIVAL AREA had gotten insanely crowded, Matt noted, with the fleeting hope that the limbo contest had reached capacity. Candy was indomitable, however, and managed to work her way to the sign-up just before they closed it off.

Hooray.

The limbo uprights were tiki torches painted to resemble bamboo, with bar rests that could be set as low as six inches from the ground. Who could possibly bend that low? Maybe Candy who was as limber as she was graceful.

Matt sighed and lined up with Candy and the other contestants. He kept catching guys checking her out. It was annoying, but he understood. Candy drew the eye. She had a great shape, of course, which the white bikini emphasized, and her dark hair gleamed in the torch-light, but there was more to it. She gave off electricity; she stood out.

He kept picturing her naked. Other guys were doing the same thing, but only he knew exactly what she looked like.

Stop.

Luckily, "Limbo Rock" blared from nearby speakers, signaling the start of the contest. The bar was high enough that most people, including him, moved easily under it. Candy went before him, lightning quick. He managed the next round, but not without effort. Several guys dropped to the sand.

The third round, he watched Candy pass under the bar, following the swell of her thigh muscles to the place where her legs met, the spot he'd touched, the space he'd entered.

Ouch. He was about to stack wood in public.

"How low can you go?" the announcer said.

That low, evidently. He couldn't stop thinking about her. She confused and overwhelmed him. He preferred his feelings to be simple and rational.

The way they'd been with Jane. She didn't slip constantly into his awareness, invade every thought, torture every nerve. With Jane, he knew what to expect. Candy would be impossible to predict. Or ignore.

"Matt? Hello?" Candy was calling him. "Your turn?"

"Oh, right. Yeah." He bent back, inched under the bar, caught sight of Candy's face and lost all strength in his legs. He hit the sand, kicking up dust.

"You had it. What happened to you?" she said, giving him a hand up.

You. You happened to me. "I don't know," he said.

He felt a little better about blowing it when most of the men and half the women were eliminated that round. Before long, Candy was among the dozen contenders left.

Then it got hard. The contestants had to go under the bar backward. It looked like agony. Player after player tumbled to the sand.

When it was Candy's turn, she inched toward the bar, her features pinched in concentration, hair swinging, her muscles tight, thighs quivering from the strain. She made that round and the next, too, her determination as palpable as the sweat that gleamed on her skin. As with the karaoke contest, the crowd loved her.

In the end she managed third place, beaten by two contortionists who defied gravity.

"You were amazing," he said, giving her a quick hug. "Let's go."

"Not so fast. There's a couples-only contest. With belly shots."

"Belly shots?" he said, his heart sinking.

She pointed at the demonstration, where a woman bent back while her partner placed a shot of tequila on her belly. She moved under the bar, he met her on the other side, picked up the shot glass with his teeth and drank it, no hands.

"We're winning it," Candy said, leveling her gaze at him. "So no backing out."

"I wouldn't think of it," he said, happy they were the last couple in the line for this particular torture. One after another the pairs tried and failed—tipping over the shot glass, bumping the bar or falling flat.

Then it was their turn.

"We're going to make it, Matt. Don't worry," she said.

"Oh, I'm not," he said, setting the shot glass on her trembling stomach before hurrying around to wait for her to inch her way under the bar toward him.

Her muscles clenched and released as she moved, glistening in the tiki light. The glass jiggled and a few drops of tequila trickled across her stomach. The audience moaned.

Her toes gripped the sand, her body vibrated from the strain, then she steadied herself.

Somehow, inch by inch, she made it beyond the bar. Now he did his part. He lowered his mouth to the shaking shot glass, picking up the scent of her skin, her light sweat and the tang of tequila. He lifted the edge with his teeth, tipped back the ounce of booze and gulped it down.

A cheer went up. Candy bounced up and he caught her against him. "We won! We won!" she shrieked, dancing and jumping like the tiki flames. The announcer handed Candy the trophy, and she held it up, her eyes shining with joy.

Matt wanted to help her celebrate, so he crouched before her and tapped his shoulders. "Climb up."

She put her legs around his neck, her thighs tight against his ears. He held her securely and stood tall.

She shrieked in pleasure. The crowd bellowed its approval. Alcohol-induced hilarity, no doubt. They'd hardly won the Olympics, but Candy was a wonder and even the drunken festival revelers had picked up on it.

"This is so great," she said, talking down to him, the trophy in one hand, her other hand under his jaw, holding on.

"Yeah," he said, looking up at her.

"Hello!"

He looked down to see Jaycee calling to him.

"Congratulations, you two," she said, glancing up at Candy, then directly at him.

"Thanks," Candy called down.

"So, anyway, I'm just going to come right out and ask. I know you two work together, but are you together-together?" She twined two fingers.

They both answered at once.

"Not at all," Candy said.

"Yes, we are," he said.

Hands on hips, Jaycee looked from one to the other, waiting for a clarification.

"For this week, we're together," he said.

"Oh. Well." She looked disappointed, then shrugged. "Whatever. I guess I'll see you around." She walked away, paused to look back, as if to say something else, then shook her head and moved on.

He understood her confusion. Why had he lied? Because he didn't want Jaycee and it was a painless way to let her down? That made sense, right?

Except there was more to it, he knew. Way more.

Candy thumped his chest with her heels. "Put me down," she said. She wanted an explanation and he hoped to God she'd buy the one he gave her.

CANDY HOPED TO HELL Matt could fix this. He had to save her from herself. When he'd told Jaycee they were *together,* she'd felt pure joy.

Joy! The absolute wrong reaction. She had to force it down, like sitting on the lid of a jam-packed suitcase. She had no business wanting Matt to want her.

Now, her heart banged her ribs as hard as her heels thudded Matt's chest.

Matt crouched down and helped her off his shoulders. She hated to leave, actually. She'd loved being up there with Matt's hands warm and tight on her thighs, holding her safe.

"Why did you tell her that?" she asked him, her heart thudding in her ears.

"I didn't want to hurt her feelings."

"You could beta test Fun Guy with her. Wasn't she your type?" she asked. How could she not be? Jaycee was every guy's type.

"Right," he said, sounding relieved. "She's not my type." His eyes darted away.

"Or is it because of Jane? Sure. That makes sense." Matt was an honorable guy. He wouldn't two-time his girlfriend. Even if she wasn't his girlfriend at the moment.

Because if it wasn't, if Matt had turned down Jaycee because he wanted Candy, then the joy she'd locked away would burst right out of her.

"This trip's complicated enough already," Matt said, managing a smile. "Don't you think?"

"Excellent point," she said, relieved Matt had eased the tension. She noticed carnival rides—their neon trim decorating the sky—in the distance, where the crowd thickened. "Let's check out the carnival before the scavenger hunt, huh?" That would be a fun distraction.

"Sounds good."

She put the limbo trophy inside her straw bag, Matt put his shirt back on, and they started off.

"Hey there…" A blond guy spoke invitingly to Candy as he passed. He turned, walking backward to continue looking at her.

She smiled her thanks-but-no-thanks smile.

Matt stopped walking and turned to her. "If you want to hook up with him, feel free. I can amuse myself."

"Forget it, Matt." She laughed.

"This is your vacation. You should do your thing."

His words hit like a slap. "You think that's my *thing*—picking up guys?"

"No. I just meant enjoy yourself, do what you want."

"I always do," she said, sounding more stiff than she meant to. It hurt that Matt saw her as a party girl.

On the other hand, why wouldn't he? She'd jumped into bed with him practically at the first chance she got.

"Stop." He surprised her by cupping her face and looking straight into her eyes. "I was clumsy. I just mean I don't want to monopolize your time. If you meet someone, I'll back off. That's all I'm saying."

Her anger melted away. "I'm having a great time with you." The words came out too intimate and too intense.

"Me, too," he said, matching her tone. "A great time." He held her gaze. "Too great, probably."

"Probably." Her heart throbbed in her chest and some joy leaked out. Why did he have to be so damned sincere?

She loved being with him, the way he looked after her, smiled at every funny remark, found her so delightful. This was not good. Not good at all.

She hurried forward, so Matt had to lope to catch up with her in the crowded midway. People were clumped around booths related to *Sin on the Beach.* A photo booth had life-size cardboard stand-ups of the stars, faces cut out, so couples could peek through and be photographed as if they were making love. Long lines

snaked around tables where the actors autographed pub-
licity photos and tell-alls.

Candy and Matt pushed past all that to a more open
section of the carnival.

"Hey there, young lovers!"

Candy turned to locate the source of the amplified
voice.

"Yes! You! White bikini, blue palm-tree shirt. I'm
talking to you." A man wearing a lime-green turban and
an eye-popping Hawaiian shirt was waving them over.
His twinkling eyes and handlebar moustache made him
look like a tall Wizard of Oz.

"Please, you two beautiful people, step this way."
Above him, a painted sign said, "Magellan the All
Knowing."

"I don't know about this," Matt muttered to her.

"Let's see what he's got to say." She tugged Matt's
arm, pulling him closer to the small stage.

"Folks, help me encourage this lovely couple,"
Magellan called to the passing crowd. "Don't let them
escape their future. I must unravel their mystery."

A dozen people gathered around the platform and
watched Matt help Candy up the steps to stand beside
the guy.

"Welcome, welcome," Magellan said. "Give them a
hand."

The crowd obediently applauded. There was a des-
ultory whistle.

"And your first name?" Magellan held the mic
close to Candy.

"Candy," she said.

"Exactly what I was going to say!" He winked at the crowd, then turned to Matt. "And you, sir? Your name is…hmm. It's…"

"Matt."

"Ah. You're too quick for me." The crowd laughed at his pretense that he'd been about to guess their names.

"And are you enjoying the festival, Matt and Candy?"

"Until now," Matt joked.

"Not to worry," Magellan said with a big laugh. "You'll be able to live this down…eventually."

The crowd laughed.

"So, ready to play our game? It's called Truth or…Bare. A variation of Truth or Dare in honor of this sexy festival we're part of."

"That depends on what we have to do," Candy said.

"Exactly," Matt added.

"You can trust me," he said. Something in his tone told her he was more than a carnie clowning for the crowd. And his eyes held a surprising depth.

"We're listening," Candy said.

"Good. Excellent." He rubbed his hands together. "Here's how it goes. I'm going to call on my spirit guides to reveal a secret about each of you. If I'm wrong, you earn fifty festival points and free tickets for the carnival rides." He pulled a strip of tickets from a pocket and waved it for the crowd's benefit.

"And if you're right?" Matt asked.

"Then it gets interesting. If I'm correct, you remove an item of clothing. A major item. No jewelry or shoes. That's why we call it Truth or *Bare*."

The crowd roared its appreciation.

"So, are you in?" he asked, looking from Matt to Candy.

No way would Candy drop her bikini for a crowd, but she was curious about what Magellan might guess. Matt looked as though he wanted to bolt from the stage. That made her smile. She liked seeing him off-guard. "Why not?" she said.

"Candy," he said under his breath.

"Relax, Fun Guy. It'll be fine." She turned to Magellan. "We're in," she said, holding out her hand.

"You're very brave." Somberly, Magellan shook her hand.

"Hang on," Matt said. He whipped off his shirt and put it around Candy's shoulders. "*Now* we're in."

The crowd booed.

"That's all well and good, my man. Quite heroic of you. However, if I guess correctly about you, you'll be in the altogether."

"I'll take my chances," Matt said, crossing his arms over his bare chest. Oooh, he looked good. Candy sighed.

"Suit yourself," Magellan said. "Or un-suit yourself, as the case may be. What do we think about that, ladies?" He directed the microphone at the crowd, where women shrieked their approval of the possibility of Matt losing his swimsuit.

"You okay with this?" Matt asked her.

"If you are," she said, impressed by his boldness. Should Magellan stumble onto a real secret, he could deny it, of course. She was sure that not even a double Tsunami for Two could convince Matt to strip in public.

"Now, if I could have a moment of silence while I contact my spirit guides," Magellan said. The crowd du-

tifully quieted and the fortune teller made a big show
of closing his eyes, placing his fingers to his temples,
then putting his palms together at his heart level. In-
stantly, mystical music swelled around them. He'd
tapped a remote, no doubt, or had an assistant backstage.

After a few seconds, Magellan opened his eyes, gave
them each a Buddha-worthy smile, put a hand on each
of their shoulders and lowered his head again. The
music swelled and Candy felt a curious warmth pass
through her body, head to toe. Had to be the power of
suggestion.

After a bit, Magellan's head jerked up and the music
stopped dead. He leveled his gaze at each of them in turn.

"First, I am prompted to point out that nothing at this
festival can compete with what you two have in mind
for each other." He grinned, then turned to the audience,
which had grown substantially. "Am I right?"

The crowd hooted its pleasure.

Matt went red under his tan. Candy managed a smile.
The guy knew how to work a crowd.

"Now, for my official reading." Magellan turned to
her, meeting her gaze full on. "Here's what my guides
tell me." He paused. "You, Candy, want something from
Matt that you're afraid to ask for."

She thought immediately about the promotion, but it
could be a million things. The secret to fortune telling
was making ambiguous guesses.

"You don't really want that, by the way," Magellan
added quietly, an odd light in his eye. She felt caught
short. "So, am I right?" he said more loudly so the crowd
could hear. "Will it be Truth?" Long pause. "Or *Bare?*"

The crowd roared.

No way could she admit the truth. Matt would want to know what it was. She had no choice but to lie. "Sorry. You are incorrect," she said.

"Really?" Magellan seemed to read her fib. "Sometimes I'm wrong," he said, making a big show of giving her a strip of tickets and, from another pocket, a voucher for points. He slanted Candy a last glance, inviting her to confess, then shrugged and turned to Matt. "Let's see now, Matt." He paused. "You, Matt, have let Candy believe a falsehood for her own good." He leaned closer to Matt and whispered, "The truth will set you free, my friend."

He spoke into the microphone. "So…am I correct? Will you trade in your swimsuit for your birthday suit, Matt?"

There was a moment of silence. Matt swallowed, looking painfully uncomfortable. "Sorry, but you're wrong," Matt said in a way that made Candy think he was lying, too. *Come on,* she scolded herself. No way was Magellan psychic. He was working the crowd, making likely guesses.

"Looks like the spirits are failing me today," Magellan said. He shook his fist heavenward in mock anger, then hung his head in pretend sorrow.

The audience clapped and shouted while he handed over Matt's winnings.

Magellan shook their hands, then spoke into the microphone. "I predict a private game of Truth or Bare in your future." He winked. "Your *very near* future. Good luck to you both."

The crowd roared at the sexual implication of his words, but Candy had the feeling that Magellan wished them luck with more than the sex he was assuming they'd have.

Matt helped her off the platform and they walked into the crowd, which moved onward. "That was mortifying," he said.

"I know," she said. "You want your shirt?" She started to shrug it off.

"Keep it," he said, eyeing her body. "It's safer that way."

"For you maybe." She looked at his bare chest, wanting it against her, electricity zinging through her. Matt's eyes crackled with a matching reaction. Neither of them was safe and they both knew it. Magellan was right. Nothing out here could compare with the pleasure they'd enjoy together.

She watched him, holding her breath.

"Maybe we should call it a night," he said, as if he'd sensed the danger, too. "Just forget the festival for now."

"We can't. I promised Ellie and Sara we'd do the scavenger hunt. We're strong enough to handle this, aren't we?"

"I guess we're going to find out," he said with a sigh, taking her by the arm and moving forward.

10

CANDY SPOTTED THE Hot Shot Scavenger Hunt right away. The stage held three movie screens and was flanked by two huge inflated cell phones marked with the brand name of the sponsoring mobile-phone company.

The emcee announced that the list of Hot Shot photos would appear on the screen and also be available via text message in five minutes. All entry shots had to be sent to the contest's cell number before midnight. From the teams whose entries met the requirements, the winner would be selected based on the quality of the photos, their originality and how fast they were turned in.

Candy and Matt located Ellie and Sara standing with two men—Bill and Drew, she assumed. Just as they'd finished introducing themselves to each other, a shout rose from the crowd. They looked up to see a list of bulleted items on all three screens.

Candy scanned the list: a guy in pink boxer briefs, a woman in a plain white bra, three women in descending cup sizes—double points if they were topless—naked female backsides with and without tan lines, a male butt cheek with a beauty or birth mark, innie and outie navels, a sexy tattoo, a woman's thong with something provocative written on it, a Day-Glo condom and more. Twenty items in all. It was dizzying.

"This is worse than I thought," Matt said, looking at her. "Pink briefs?"

"Okay, quick. Innie or outie?" Ellie asked the group, undaunted by the challenge. In seconds, Drew's and Sara's navels had been photographed—he was innie, she was outie—and Candy and her friends had divvied up the rest of the shots.

Matt waited, nervous as hell, Candy could see.

"We got the easy stuff, don't sweat it," she told him. The scavenger hunt crowd had dissipated in search of photographic victims, so Candy dragged Matt over to a group of easygoing-looking guys she hoped to convince to be their Three Moons Over Malibu shot.

The guys were happy to oblige. Matt looked stunned while she captured the picture.

Next, she led him to five women drinking from novelty glasses—a clue they were in get-drunk-go-crazy mode. In no time at all, Candy had three of them lined up in cup order—D, C, A.

"Now, when I say flash, lift your tops," she said.

Matt looked away politely when the girls did as she'd asked, and Candy took their picture.

Afterward, they gave her a cell number so she could send them the photo.

"I can't believe how easily you talk people out of their clothes," Matt said, sounding honestly awed.

"What can I say? It's a gift."

She sent the shots to Ellie's and Sara's phones, saw what they'd snapped, then grinned at Matt. "We're on target. The rest of our shots are easy. We'll grab glow-in-the-dark condoms at Walgreens, you've got the ass with a beauty mark and I've got the sexy thong. Come on." She took his arm.

"Hold it. I have a beauty mark on my—?"

"Left butt cheek, yes. Didn't you know? It matches this one." She tapped the spot on his right cheek.

He touched it, brushing her finger.

"The one on your backside stands out because you're pale back there. Maybe consider nude sunbathing. Or a tanning bed."

He lifted his eyebrows. She loved to shock him.

"Come on," she said, tugging at him.

"Wait a sec." He stopped dead. "I'm not dropping my pants in public for you to photograph."

"No problem. We have to go to my place for the thong anyway."

"Candy, do you realize they're going to show these photos up there?" He nodded toward the huge screens on stage.

"It'll be fine. Just your butt and only my underwear. No identifying features. It's modeling. Come on."

"I can't believe I'm letting you talk me into this," he said, moving into a trot to keep up with her.

"It's for a good cause."

"Good thing you're not offering swampland. It seems I'm buying whatever you're selling."

Once they'd nabbed and photographed a packet of neon condoms and sent the shot to the girls, Candy unlocked the door to the beach house and led Matt inside.

She flipped on the lights, then faced him, cell phone

ready. "Okay, show me what you got, big boy." She was trying for a jokey tone, but her voice shook.

"You said the left cheek?" When she nodded, he turned away, slid his thumb into his trunks and shoved them down, revealing the muscled swell of his gorgeous ass. He looked over his shoulder. "How's that?"

"Perfect." It was like some hot Calvin Klein ad and she felt such a rush of arousal she could hardly click the picture. In fact, the first one blurred.

"One more," she said, holding her breath and stilling her shaking long enough to snap the shot.

She showed it to him. "Like I said. I'm the only one who can tell it's you."

"You can tell?" he said gruffly.

"How could I forget how you look naked?" she breathed, swaying closer.

No, no, no. Stick to the goal—get the shots, then go.

"Hold this while I get my thong." She handed him the phone, then went to paw through her suitcase for the novelty underwear, which she waved at Matt. "I'll put this on and be right back."

"I'll wait," he said slowly, one hand fisting at his side, the other holding the camera.

The moment that had started out so matter-of-fact was now a rising tide of heat that lifted Candy off her feet. She could see in Matt's eyes he felt the same.

They were all alone in the house and nearly naked. SyncUp seemed far away. Everything in her was demanding she do something about this before she burst into flames on the spot.

She rushed to the bathroom, slammed the door and leaned on it, her heart in her throat, fighting for air and some trace of good sense, which seemed to have fled the scene.

She had the terrible thought that the *near future* Magellan had predicted for them was right here, right now.

THIS WAS TOO SURREAL for words. Candy was in the bathroom donning the tiniest strip of fabric known to man so that Matt could take her picture in it. How had he gotten here?

Already, he'd allowed her to photograph his bare ass to be flashed on a huge screen for thousands of strangers.

And he wasn't sorry. Or not very sorry. Yet.

He wasn't drunk this time. He'd had wine and sucked a shot of tequila from Candy's belly, but that had been hours ago. Just in case, he tried standing on one leg and touching his nose. He was sober, all right. No, his problem wasn't alcohol. It was the wild enzymes that flooded the human brain when it was aroused, ready to fight or flee or ask a girl to marry him.

All because of Candy, that willful whirlwind who had strangers cheerfully whipping off their underwear at her whim.

No wonder he'd ended up here. She was the most charming woman he'd ever met, a ball of energy and fun he wanted to hold on to for dear life.

There was something going on here. Something he didn't want to miss. He felt himself focus, felt his energy concentrate to a pinpoint of attention. This was his way, he knew, his tendency to push hard toward a goal, not to be deterred until he had what he wanted.

And what he wanted right now was Candy.

Forget SyncUp, forget his good sense, forget his career, his duty. Forget everything but this moment.

Something important was happening to him or at least that's how it seemed. Before he could close in on whether or not he was delusional, the door opened and there stood Candy.

She seemed to glow, rim-lit somehow. He realized that when he was with her, the world seemed more vivid. He noticed things he usually ignored—the shifting colors of sunset, the grind of sand under his soles, the way the heat of the sun crawled like goose bumps across his shoulders, the blur and shimmer of seaside light and the way her husky laugh lit him up inside.

She wore the white bikini top and, below, a tiny triangle of black cloth with a red X over Marks the Spot in lacy script.

X marks the spot. Yeah. The spot he'd touched last night. He'd held his thumb there and made her moan with pleasure. He wanted to do that again. He wanted to surprise her, please her, make her scream.

Lust surged through him in a wave that threatened to drown him if he didn't go along for the ride.

"You ready?" she asked, walking closer.

"Oh, yeah," he breathed. "I'm ready."

"Your phone?" She smiled tentatively at him, then looked around, spotting her cell phone on the table. "You can use mine." She handed it to him. "Did you forget why we're here?" She bit her lip, uncertain.

"Not at all." He took the phone, but kept watching her, fighting for control, giving restraint one last chance.

"Where do you want me?" she said, her voice shaky.

"Anywhere you want to be."

She positioned herself with her legs wide, her hands on her hips, most of her body bared to his gaze. "How about here?"

He looked at her through the viewer.

"Can you read the words on the thong? They need to be clear. Maybe take it at eye level?"

"I don't think you know what you're asking." He dropped to his knees, inches away, eye level with the X. His cock jutted outward in his trunks. If she looked down, she'd see.

He realized he wanted her to know what she did to him.

He took the shot, caught up in being so close to her. Her stomach quivered and he picked up her light musk, heady and arousing. He was a strip of cloth away from heaven.

And he was suddenly sick of hell. He'd had it with fighting the flames. Time to put out the fire.

"Enough." He shut the phone and tossed it to the couch. "Forget the contest and the deal." He grabbed Candy's hips and looked up into her face.

Her eyes widened in alarm, but they gleamed too, with the same desire that burned through him.

There were no words now, only actions. He pressed his tongue against her through the fabric.

She quivered against him, sinking down. "What are you doing?"

Making you mine flew through his mind.

"But you can't… You…oh. Don't… Oh, yes…"

He nuzzled her, then blew a breath, before moving his tongue up and down over the panties, wet now from his saliva and the juices he could taste, sweet and salty at once.

"We *agreeed*." She moaned, grabbing his hair, struggling for balance.

He'd stop if she truly wanted him to. But then she leaned into his mouth and nudged her sex against his lips, asking for more.

Which he was happy to give. He gripped her hips, held her closer, pressed harder with his tongue. She moaned and her thighs trembled against his cheeks.

He wanted the thong gone, so he tugged it down and ran his tongue over her swollen clit hiding beneath soft curls.

She squealed. "Oh, that is so…oh…oh…don't…ever…*stooop*."

He reached behind her and cupped her bottom, angling her so his tongue could reach her opening. He pressed down the way she'd liked his fingers pushing in last night. He was so hard he was blind to anything but this moment, her body, her musk, her sounds. He wanted inside, too, but first this.

He ran his tongue down her length and reached inside.

"Oh, oh, oh." She rocked against him and he felt the pulse of her need against his tongue. She was swollen, ready to fly with just a bit more—a slide of his tongue, a burst of hot breath. He gave her both.

She stilled and said his name as if he were everything to her. And for this moment, he wanted to be. He pushed his tongue into her as far as he could. She rocked wildly and cried out, caught on the wave of her release. He held her, stayed with her, felt the rhythmic flutter of her spasms.

When she was done, he kissed her hair, then rose to his feet. Holding her with one arm, he used his other hand to rid himself of his trunks.

Reading what he wanted, Candy gave a little jump, then wrapped her legs around his waist, her arms around his neck.

He carried her to the closest wall, braced her, opened her and entered her slickness with one hard stroke.

"You feel so *good,*" she said on a moan.

He thrust up, loving the way she gripped him with her sex and her arms. He cupped her bottom, supporting her as best he could, burying himself deep, never wanting to leave the tight warm space she'd opened to him.

His heart seemed to be pounding a hole in his ribs. He'd become a mindless creature, backing her into a wall to have her. Not civilized, not sensible, completely out of control.

He didn't care. He had to claim her, make her his.

Their eyes met. Hers glittered with the same frantic need he felt and her breath rasped, as if she fought for air. They were in this together, this crazy place where they were like that tsunami of liquor in each other's bloodstream—gushing, rushing, sweeping away everything in its path.

His climax approached. He tightened, then paused, letting the feeling build, waiting to see where Candy was.

"Don't stop...I'm...there," she said, locking her knees around him. When he thrust again, she said his name and he smiled into her hair.

They shuddered and shook together. Spilling into her, he let go of a tension he hadn't realized he'd carried. For a blinding second, he felt free, light as air, and he realized he wanted to laugh out loud.

He lifted her away from the wall. She let her arms flop over his back and panted near his ear.

"Where's your bed?" he murmured to her.

"The foldout," she gasped. "But let's borrow one upstairs."

He turned for the stairs.

"Wait," she said. "Bend down."

He did and she scooped up the phone. "I've got to send the shots to Ellie and Sara."

He was amazed she could manage any task at all, but while he carried her to the first bedroom and yanked down the spread, she thumbed away at the phone.

He laid her down on the bed.

"There," she said on a sigh, extending her arm to the side and letting the phone drop. "I hope we win."

"Who cares? All I want is you." He took off her bikini top, cupped her breast and ran his tongue around each nipple while she squirmed under him.

After a few more seconds, she gripped his face and with what seemed like a tremendous effort, lifted him away from her breasts. "What are we doing, Matt?" she moaned.

"I can't fight this anymore." He kissed her sweet mouth, hiding from his conscience in the rush of rightness he felt whenever he embraced her.

"I know. I feel the same way, but this is wrong. We have to figure out how it can be right." She seemed close to tears.

He forced himself to calm down, to think. "Okay. We know the danger. We can't let this change anything at work. Can you do that, do you think?"

Her eyes flew across his face and he could see her mind working frantically, assessing, deciding. "I think so. This is vacation, right?"

"And I'm not myself, remember? I'm Fun Guy?" It sounded ridiculous, but he'd say anything to keep her naked. "What happens in Malibu…" So lame.

But she didn't call him on it. In fact, she smiled. "And our deal stays the same. You'll consider my marketing plan on its merits? Keep this, what we're doing, separate?"

"Sure. Of course." He saw the doubt in her eyes. "Let's add this to the deal. You're teaching me to be more social."

"Come on. I'm giving you sex lessons?" She tilted her head, grinning. Good. She was accepting this. Her body softened.

"Please," she said in a low, teasing voice. "That tongue thing…whew…you've earned your PhD."

"Everyone needs a refresher." He kissed her deep, letting his tongue explore the soft insides of her mouth. "Be gentle with me."

She laughed, a throaty chuckle that turned his insides liquid. This woman knew fun in every fiber of her being. He *could* learn from her. He kissed her neck and ran his fingers across her nipple until she shivered and moaned.

"So, we're getting it out of our systems?" She seemed to struggle to get out the words, to work out the rationale.

"Completely."

"And when we get back, everything's the same."

"Absolutely." He knew he'd say yes to anything right now. They'd made it sound simple, but he wasn't so sure. "This is a unique situation, a phenomenon."

"What? Like the aurora borealis?"

"Exactly. Like a comet visible only once in a lifetime."

She laughed. "If you start on the seven wonders of the world, I'm leaving."

"Whatever gets you in." He'd made it sound like a joke, but that was truly how he felt.

"I'm in," she said softly, then slowly rose to straddle him. "And now I want you there. In. Me."

"Just what I was thinking." He found his way into her body and it was everything he wanted at the moment. Their being together was like some natural wonder—a startling comet that zipped by so fast you wondered if you'd seen it at all.

11

THE NEXT MORNING, CANDY woke early to the sound of Matt breathing in her ear. She smiled, enjoying the warm heaviness of his body overlapping hers. She pressed her nose against his forearm and inhaled deeply of the cozy smell of his skin.

After deciding on their fling, they'd returned to his place and made love over and over. She thought about how Matt had tirelessly tracked her pleasure each time. At midnight, they'd stopped for sustenance—an entire box of HoHos and a quart of Dr. Pepper—then engaged in a pillow fight that collapsed into soft, slow lovemaking. She felt so good with him, so close to him. This *had* to be okay.

A vacation fling was the perfect solution, wasn't it?

She fought the part of her that felt weak and defeated, that knew she'd succumbed to her spoiled ways, chosen short-term fun over long-term investment, done what made her feel good, not what was good for her.

Except when she looked over at Matt, she experienced such a rush of happiness she *had* to believe this was right. She believed in living life fully, seizing experiences, right? This was too intense to pass up.

Matt would still look at her Ledger Lite plan, after all, and she would still teach him networking. And wasn't this better than returning to SyncUp with lust still throbbing between them?

But what if they didn't get past it? What if they still wanted each other desperately? What if this changed everything? Her stomach burned at the thought.

They had to finish it here. Had to. She tried to calm herself down with a reality check. Once Matt got back to SyncUp, Fun Guy would disappear. The old Matt had been resistible enough. And, workaholic that he was, Matt would naturally turn his intense focus away from her and back to the job. The flame would be out like a windblown pilot light.

She knew how to prove she was still in control of herself. Today, she would work. They had no festival-event obligations, so she'd go back to the beach house and flesh out the Ledger Lite marketing plan, then invite Matt over to see it. Work, then play. Perfect. Sensible. Proof that the new, more mature Candy was still the boss.

She wiggled out from under Matt without waking him, leaving him a note that promised a call when she was ready for him to see what she'd done.

At the beach house, she tiptoed onto the porch only to find Sara carefully sliding her key in the lock, hair tousled, shoes in hand, wearing an oversize T-shirt, clearly trying to sneak in soundlessly.

Candy motioned her away from the door. "Looks like you had an interesting night," she whispered, nodding at Sara's clothes. At the scavenger hunt, Sara had had on the red halter dress Candy had loaned her. "Wasn't Drew wearing that last night?"

"Yes. It's his." Sara blushed, then fumbled in her bag for Candy's dress, which she held out. "Thanks so much. I'll have it cleaned for you."

"No, you won't. If it helped you end up like that—" she nodded at the shirt, which hit Sara mid-thigh "—it's worth every crease." Candy shoved the dress into her bag.

"So what happened?" she whispered.

"It's a long story."

"I've got time."

"And I've got coffee."

They whirled to find Ellie in the open doorway holding out two steaming mugs of coffee. "It's my blend, girls. Come inside and tell me everything. I've got warm ruglah, too."

Candy and Sara took the coffee and followed Ellie into the kitchen, where the cinnamon smell of the pastry mingled with the rich Guatemalan-Columbian blend Ellie favored.

They wiggled onto bar stools and began talking, practically at once. First, they discussed the outcome of the Hot Shot contest. They'd been beaten by a team that Sara had caught faking a birthmark. They agreed to watch out for those guys.

They moved on to how the wet T-shirt photo had resulted in Sara's putting on Drew's shirt and wading into the ocean. Sara turned three shades of peach explaining how they got *distracted* in the water. *At length*.

Afterward, Candy hugged her. "I'm so proud of you, girl."

"This isn't like me at all," Sara said.

"That's the point of being here—to be different," Candy said.

"Speaking of being different," Ellie said. "It's your turn. Tell us again about how you and Matt will never be a notch on my matchmaker's belt."

"It's actually quite sensible," Candy started, breaking out in a sweat, hoping her friends would see the sense of the plan. "We just added sex to our, um, work deal. It's a vacation affair that won't change anything. In fact, right now I'm going to work up a marketing plan I promised to show him later."

"Hold it." Ellie stared at her. "You and my brother made mad hot love last night and this morning you're *working?*" She looked at Sara. "Is she channeling you now?"

"It fits, don't you see?" Candy continued. "What better way to prove to Matt that I can work as hard as I play?"

Ellie and Sara looked at each other, not buying it one bit.

She had to change the subject. "We told you our stories, El. What about you and Bill? How did you two make out?"

"Exactly," she said. "We did make out. On the Ferris wheel. It was so…sexy and…romantic…and…I don't know…"

"That's all you did? Make out?"

Ellie blushed, something Candy had never seen before—maybe Ellie's goth makeup hid the color. "Uh-huh…that's all." She picked up a spoon and stirred her coffee for a moment. "And who knows what will happen tonight, after the shoot? We're getting together."

Candy had never seen Ellie so breathless.

"We want the full scoop later, don't we, Sara?"

"You'd better hurry up, El. You're lagging the team," Sara said. "We've both, um, gotten laid." That expression was so *not* the ever-polite Sara that Candy laughed out loud. She looked from the sex-fresh Sara to the beaming Ellie. "I love seeing you two like this." Despite whatever mess she'd gotten into with Matt, being here when her friends spread their sexual wings made the trip worth everything.

Ellie went to get dressed for *Sin on the Beach,* Sara readied for her surf lesson with Drew—distracted momentarily by a call from her uncle—and Candy got busy on Matt's computer.

She sketched a draft plan, then called the office to fill in the blanks. She got the research department to send her the data showing that Ledger Lite's market had maxed out, got verification that their payroll software customers would be a prime market, and found a programmer who thought he could adapt the interface from a math-education product to Ledger Lite Personal.

She even had Freeda e-mail her a copy of the strategic plan so she could see where her product would fit. She found the document endless, complex and dull. Who wrote this shit?

The managers, she realized. As a team leader, she'd be part of creating this damn thing every year. That would not be her favorite part of the job, for sure.

Who could enjoy it? She'd get used to it, though. The managers probably sucked it up and did it. She'd just figure out a way to make it fun.

That was what she brought to the table.

A few minor irritations were nothing compared with the rewards of the promotion. She couldn't wait to announce it at the family Thanksgiving dinner—when they went around the table and said what they were most grateful for.

After that, no more paternal glances over her head or brotherly sighs behind her back. They'd see she was making progress, sticking with something, not floating aimlessly from job to job. For that moment of glory, she could handle a few meetings and some boring reports.

When she logged into e-mail, she got a reminder beep from her calendar and saw that the women's business association's luncheon was tomorrow. It was their awards celebration. Now *that* was a crowd that would love Ledger Lite Personal.

Which gave her a perfect idea—she'd go to the luncheon and bring Matt for a networking lesson. That would impress him with her networking savvy *and* her devotion to SyncUp. She stretched her arms up and rubbed her neck and back, tired from sitting so long.

A woof made her look toward the screen door. Matt stood with Radar. "Enough work," Matt said, coming inside, leaving Radar on the porch.

"Not quite," she said. "I have a great idea. There's a business luncheon tomorrow and I want you to come with me and do some networking."

"We're on vacation, Candy." He came to stand behind her and nuzzle her neck. Goose bumps shot down her arm. The dog whined outside. "I had ten messages on my cell from work. Guess what I'm doing about that?"

She turned to him for his answer.

"Not a thing."

"Do you think that's wise?"

"I don't care." He leaned down to kiss her. "Forget work. Forget luncheons. I want you in bed."

His urgency sent hot fire zooming through her. "First, promise you'll come to the lunch tomorrow."

"You drive a hard bargain." He ran his thumbs across her nipples through her top, making her shiver.

"Do you want to see what I've got so far?"

"Oh, yeah," he said, but he wasn't talking about Ledger Lite's marketing plan. He kissed down her neck, running his tongue across a tendon in a way that melted her to butter. "Show me what you've got." He lifted her out of her chair.

She loved it and wanted to dissolve into his arms, but she had to stick to her plan. Somehow. "I had a thought about building Paycheck Plus sales, too," she said, knowing she'd never get him to look at the computer.

"Hmmm?" He seemed to struggle to focus.

"We need to boost word-of-mouth with a wow moment."

"Okay…" He stopped kissing her, but his mouth was dangerously close.

"The software is so great, so easy to use, that users take it for granted," she said, gaining enthusiasm as she spoke. "It needs a whiz-bang hook for users to buzz about."

"Sure," he said, running his hands down her arms, reaching around to grasp her bottom.

"That's the incredible thing. It *has* a whiz-bang hook.

Gina told me about a tickler alarm that no one uses because it's buried in the manual."

"Yeah?" He stopped moving his fingers.

"When they find it, people love it. It's a little complex, but if we set up a podcast for key contacts and show them the steps, they'll talk it up for us." Noticing his dreamy expression, she stopped. "Are you even listening?"

"Sure. I'm listening…and watching your lips…and kissing you." He kissed her, slow and steady. "And thinking about making love to you. Multitasking." He pulled her close and pressed himself against her, stoking the heat building inside her.

"You're catching on," she breathed, kissing him back. She'd accomplished enough to take a break, right? "So what do you think of my idea about the podcast?"

"It's great. All your ideas are great," he murmured.

"I have another one," she said, breaking away long enough to lock the door for privacy, though Ellie and Sara would be out for hours. The dog, meanwhile, had given up on them.

Returning to where Matt stood, Candy sat on the sofa and pulled him close, running her palm along his erection through his trunks.

Matt took a rough breath.

She slid his suit down to his ankles and grasped his cock.

"Like I said," Matt breathed, "I like *all* your ideas."

She gave him a long, slow lick before closing her lips around the head of his cock, taking him deep into her mouth.

"Ah, Candy." The reverent whisper turned her on. He

was warm and tasted of salt and man and she loved the way he put his hands to her face as she worked over him.

She relaxed her throat and sucked him deeper until he groaned in pleasurable agony.

He stroked her hair, while she sucked and tugged, cupping his balls in one hand, using her other to grip his shaft low and tight.

In a few moments, he stilled, ready to come. She gave a last pull, her lips tight, her fingers squeezing low, inviting him to spurt into her mouth.

She swallowed his warm fluid, then looked up at him.

His face was so full of feeling, she was startled. It was more than pleasure. It was connection, closeness, a new intimacy that she realized she felt, too.

Matt helped her up and into his arms and he kissed her softly, holding her close, telling her with his arms and lips how much she meant to him.

Together, they unfolded the couch to reveal the bed, then stripped each other until they lay face-to-face. Matt ran a hand down the side of her body, then found where she ached and stroked her until she was moaning and sliding against his fingers.

He entered her then and her body stretched to take him in, eager for each thrust and slide. Together they climbed toward the peak, each stroke bringing them closer and closer. She never wanted this to be over.

Her orgasm pushed through her in a hot, hard wave. Matt surged into her, her name on his lips. She collapsed against him, feeling his heart pound against her chest.

This was so nice. Heaven.

But even heaven got old, right?

After they recovered, Matt suggested they go for a swim.

"I'll get my suit," she said, pushing out of the bed to bend over her suitcase.

Matt stood behind her, looking on. "Wear the white one," he said, cupping her backside possessively, running his tongue along her ear. "It looks good against your skin. And those strings make you easy to get to." He ran his fingers down her slit, making her feel faint.

Somehow, they both managed to put their suits on and head out. They found Radar on the beach, as if he was waiting for them, and played with him for a while, enjoying the breeze, the waves, the seagulls' calls, the warm sun.

Then they swam, beyond nearly everyone. Candy felt so strong, she thought she could swim to the next beach town. They stopped at the reef where they'd stood that first night. Matt dived down.

She felt a tug on both sides of her suit bottom, then it was gone, and Matt rose with it in his teeth.

"Matt!" She looked around, hoping no one could see.

He took it out of his mouth. "You're safe. I checked." Then he found her with his fingers. "Mmm. How's that?"

"Lovely," she said, practically losing feeling in her legs.

"No shrieking, now, or a lifeguard might try to save you."

"I don't want to be saved," she said. "Ever." Pleasure built in waves like the ocean that passed by them, lifting, then setting them down again together.

When her climax hit, Candy put her mouth on Matt's

shoulder to muffle her cry and clung to him, wrapping her legs around his body, so happy to be with him like this.

"That was nice," he said, kissing her, cuddling her close. "How about some sun?" They returned to shore and found a sheltered area too rocky for swimmers, where they spread their big, blue-striped towels between protective boulders.

Matt fished the sunscreen from her bag and massaged the warm liquid into her back and legs.

When it was her turn, she worked the cream into his back and, when he turned over, his chest and thighs, aware that his erection was mere inches from her fingers.

So tempting.

Checking to be sure no one could see them, she slid her fingers into his trunks and stroked him.

He turned lowered eyes her way. "You'll get us arrested," he said lazily.

"Not if you're quiet," she said.

"I'll do my best." His face tightened with the pleasure of what she was doing to him.

She rubbed him in earnest, leaning over him to hide her movements. His eyes glittered with pleasure and he watched her as she slid her fingers up and down, over and over, feeling him tighten and tense. When he reached climax, she shifted the towel to catch his release.

"That was great," he said, pulling her onto his body.

"Can you believe we're doing this?" She rested her chin on a fist on his chest, watching his face. The sun warmed her back, the rhythmic crash of the waves soothed her. Distant shouts and laughter were delicious punctuation to the moment.

"It seems like a dream." He ran his fingers through her hair.

"I know. Unreal."

"I've never done anything like this before."

"You mean had sex on the beach?" She grinned.

"That either," he said. "I've never been so caught up with anyone."

Not with Jane? But she wouldn't ask, didn't want to remember the other woman in his life or what she might think about their vacation fling.

"How about you?" Matt asked. "Have there been any serious guys in your life?" He ran his fingers along her cheek.

"Serious ones? Never." She joked away the question, but she could feel Matt wanted a real answer.

"You know what I mean. Boyfriends."

"On a short-term basis, sure. Nothing too major." She thought about the one time she'd been hurt. "Except there was one guy in college. Brad. We had a thing for a couple of years. We ended up friends though."

"What happened?"

"We were on and off a lot, and eventually… You know how it goes."

"No, I don't. How did it go?"

"He wanted to get married and I…didn't." Not exactly. It had been late in their senior year and they'd agreed to take another break from each other. Three weeks later, Brad was engaged to a business major he'd had classes with.

Candy had been surprisingly hurt. She hadn't wanted marriage, but if she'd known *he* did, she'd have at least moved in with him. They were alike—both with wild streaks—and they'd had a lot of fun together. In the end, she'd swallowed her pride and actually asked him, *Why not me?*

Brad had been mystified, almost laughed. *You don't want that,* he'd said. *Marriage isn't you.*

He was more or less right, but it hurt that he hadn't considered her marriage material, had simply written her off. It made her feel limited by her reputation, trapped by it.

Years later, she'd decided the problem was that she was spoiled. She wanted it all—even if it didn't suit her.

"That happens," Matt said, reading something in her face. Did she look hurt? God she hoped she was over that. "For it to work, you have to want the same thing, have compatible goals. Once you get past the heat and settle into a routine, I mean."

"Why would you want to get past the heat?" she said. "And who wants routine? Talk about killing the joy."

"There's joy in the familiar," he said. "What's life, if not the day-to-day moments?"

"But that's boring. You have to shake things up, keep each other guessing."

"I'm not surprised you'd say that. You remind me of a girlfriend I had."

"Oh, yeah?"

"Yeah. She liked to shake things up, too. As a matter of fact, she was into roller coasters."

"I can relate."

"You would have liked her," he mused.

"What happened?"

"She shook things up." He gave a wry smile. "She warned me, though. She called it *emotional ADD*. Of course, I thought I could fix her. I couldn't."

"You were young."

"Yeah." He gave a soft laugh. "So, you think you'll ever settle down?" He asked as though it would be a long shot, which gave her that locked-in feeling, that sense she was trapped by what other people thought about her.

"Sure. Why not? When the time is right."

"And the guy. He'd have to be the right guy— someone into Silly String and karaoke and the limbo. Someone who'll keep you guessing."

"You got it," she said, knowing that proved how wrong they were for each other, not that it mattered. That wasn't even on the table. She rolled off him and braced herself with her elbows.

He did the same, so they were lying side by side, looking out to sea.

"Speaking of shaking things up," he said slowly, staring at something in the sky. He pointed toward a bright spot of color. "I know what we're doing next."

She realized it was a parasail. Two people dangled there, miles high, dots with legs against the blue sky, the boat far, far below. Candy's heart lurched and she felt the swirling vertigo she got whenever she found herself on a balcony.

"You want us to parasail?" she asked, her mouth dry.

"Have you done it before? I never have."

"No, no. I haven't. Um, not yet." She swallowed over a suddenly tight throat, not wanting to admit her fear.

"Then it's perfect. Something new we can do

together." He got to his feet and reached for her hand. He seemed excited he'd found a way to shake things up.

He had no idea.

She pushed past the quiver in her stomach, the constriction in her chest, how dizzy she felt and said, "I can't wait."

Maybe it wouldn't be as scary as it looked.

MATT PAID THE SPEEDBOAT owner for a tandem parasail ride and before long they were putting on yellow life jackets while the boat zoomed out into the ocean. He grinned at Candy, delighted he'd found some thrill she'd not yet had. Then he noticed her fingers were shaking as she clicked the clasps.

"You okay?" he asked.

"I just can't get this." She fumbled the bottom latch, so he clicked it into place for her. Her smile was tentative and her face pale.

"What's wrong? Are you feeling sick?"

"I guess lunch didn't sit well in my stomach."

"Do you want to cancel? We can come back tomorrow."

"No. We're here. It'll be great. Once we get...up there." She forced a look that was as determined as her voice was weak.

Before he could pursue the contradiction, one of the crew called them to climb into the side-by-side harnesses that reminded him of a toddler's playground swing.

Matt put his hand around Candy's on her upright line, surprised to find she had the rope in a death grip. Her body was trembling, too. "Are you cold?" he asked.

She shook her head. "Just excited."

No, he realized abruptly. She was scared. How had he not noticed? "Candy, if you're nervous, we can quit right now."

"No! I'm a little jumpy about heights is all. I'll be fine once we get moving." She swallowed hard and forced a shaky smile. "This is an adventure."

"We'll do something else that doesn't upset you." He leaned forward to call to the crew.

"Don't you dare!" Candy said fiercely. She leveled her gaze at him. "I want to try this. We're going up. It's an adventure."

The guy asked if they were ready.

Candy shot him a thumbs-up and before Matt could intervene, the crewman released the winch and let out the tether. Slowly, Matt and Candy rose, up and away from the boat. It was an incredible sensation. He felt weightless and free, but he kept his gaze glued to Candy, whose eyes were shut tight.

His heart lurched. He should have stopped this. Forget her pride. No way would he allow her to be terrorized on his whim.

He was about to signal the crew to pull them in when she opened her eyes and smiled cautiously. "This is…nice." She looked gingerly around, then glanced down. That made her gasp and squeeze her eyes shut again.

"Candy, let's quit. You got up here. You proved yourself. You can say you've parasailed."

"No," she said, eyes tight, pale as milk beneath the pink of her sunburn. "Baby steps is how they fix phobias. I'm working through it. I just won't look down. Right away, anyway."

The woman was being her own therapist. "You're amazing, you know that."

"I'm just me," she said, steadying her gaze on him. The wind blew her hair away from her sweet face. She looked scared and brave, vulnerable and fierce all at once and emotion built inside him.

He watched her build up her courage, keeping her eyes open for a few more seconds each time. Before long, she let out a huge yell of triumph. "Yeah! I did it!" She released her rope long enough to squeeze his hand. "This is great. Thanks, Matt." She smiled, her eyes bright, her voice warm with gratitude.

Looking at her like this, radiant with courage and triumph, Matt's heart flipped over in his chest.

"What?" she asked him. "What's up?"

"Nothing," he said, but that wasn't true. Something was up, all right. Two-hundred feet in the air, he'd fallen for Candy.

Which was insane. And impossible. Even if they didn't work together, which was trouble enough, Matt had no interest in the emotional roller coaster that Candy would consider normal. He liked things calm and stable. She liked to shake things up. They were apples and oranges, oil and water, as she'd said. And all the lighter fluid in the world wouldn't change that.

Still, as he watched Candy laugh, head thrown back, reveling in the moment, love billowed inside him, taut and broad as the parasail that held them aloft, as if it planned to keep him in the air forever.

He knew then that it was too late for good sense, for willpower, for turning back. He was in love with Candy and now he had to figure out what to do about it.

12

CANDY LOOKED OUT across the sky, careful not to look down, thrilled to be floating on air, surrounded by blue, blue sky. She'd not only conquered her fear, but found a new thrill—parasailing. It was fantastic…electrifying… She felt so alive. And so grateful to Matt for giving her this gift.

"I love this," she said, looking right at him. *And I love you.*

Uh-oh. Bad idea. Just an overflow of her delight, right? Except Matt looked at her so warmly, it was as though she'd actually said the words and he'd said them back to her.

That was scary. She felt dizzy and faint, the way she'd expected to feel floating so far above the water, but didn't. Not anymore. She'd gotten used to it. Could she get used to these feelings for Matt?

She became suddenly aware that they'd stopped moving forward and had begun to drop in altitude. "What's happening?" she said. "Are we going down?"

"It has to end sometime," he said softly and she knew he wasn't talking just about the parasail ride.

"Too bad."

"Nothing lasts forever."

"If it did, we'd be bored or burned out."

"Probably." He sighed.

"We'll make the most of every minute," she said, determined to do just that.

The parasail crew seemed to sense their need to hang on to the experience, because they gave them an extra bit of time to dangle their feet in the water before they hauled them onto the boat, ending the trip.

They smiled at each other and tried to act as if nothing had changed. But it had, all right, and Candy could tell the end of their affair would not be as easy or simple as they'd made it sound last night.

"A BUSINESS LUNCH? And you're taking Matt?" Sara stared at Candy, as she tugged the drugstore panty hose under the single cocktail dress she'd brought on the trip. She'd borrowed a linen blazer from Sara to give the outfit some business flair.

"It's perfect. Matt gets another networking lesson, I talk up Ledger Lite Personal with possible clients and impress him even more with my professionalism." Plus, it would be a taste of being in the work world again, a chance to test their ability to keep work and play separate.

After the parasailing, they'd managed to get back more or less to how they'd been—making love for hours, laughing and talking as if nothing had changed.

Still, Candy knew she was in a fog. The mere thought of Matt started her heart banging in her chest. The luncheon, she hoped, would put things in perspective.

She pulled on the blazer and checked herself in the

mirror. Perfect. On the surface, she looked serious and sober and all business. Inside, she was squishy and soft and woozy with tenderness for Matt. She hoped her outside would rub off on her inside and not the reverse.

Ellie floated down the stairs, dressed in her new, softer clothes. Since she'd slept with Bill, she'd become positively dreamy. "What's happening?" she asked when she reached her friends.

"Candy's going to a business luncheon with Matt," Sara answered. "Welcome to the bizarro world. Candy's working all the time and all I can think of is playing with Drew."

"Isn't it wonderful?" Ellie said wistfully. "Everything worked out. You and Drew. Me and Bill. Candy and Matt." She sighed.

"It *is* great," Sara breathed. "Drew and I really connected. He truly understands me."

"I feel that way, too, with Bill," Ellie said.

Candy smiled at her dazed and confused friends. She hoped they wouldn't get hurt. It's not that she was cynical, just practical. She had to stay clear-eyed about her own situation as well. "It's not like that with me and Matt." She tugged the blazer hem, straightening out the creases.

"Oh, no. Not at all," Ellie said, wearing her know-it-all grin. "With you and Matt, it's *strictly business.*"

"I'm serious, Ellie. Really. Besides, as soon as Jane sees the new Matt, she'll want him back. I know it."

"But that's over. He doesn't want her anymore," Ellie said. "That's obvious."

"He might not say it out loud… I'm sure he doesn't want to get his hopes up." Matt was too polite to talk about Jane with her. Candy tried not to feel too guilty about them being together.

"I don't think either of you knows yourself as well as you think you do." Ellie adjusted Candy's blazer collar, which was inside out.

Candy hadn't noticed. Her vision did seem a bit foggy today. "The point is that we can't continue this when we get back. Think of it. How could Matt name me a team leader if we were sleeping together? Think how bad that would look."

"Things work out," Ellie said. "A friend of mine slept with her business partner for years before they told their employees and it was no big deal. Everyone knew and no one cared."

"At SyncUp, people would care. Trust me." Her reputation was already shaky enough there. An affair with her boss would look really, really bad. Not to mention how it would reflect on Matt.

"One of you could leave. Matt's moved around before. And don't you want your own agency anyway?"

"In five years, sure." She knew several PR and ad people who had spun off from in-house work with big firms to become consultants, with their former employers as their biggest accounts. "When I have enough experience. I'm not leaving SyncUp yet. That would be way too flaky."

"Starting your own agency is not flaky," Sara said. "You'd be your own boss, depending on yourself for your income. You'd love that, Candy. I think you'd shine."

"I know what I want. I have a plan."

"Just keep an open mind, that's all we're saying,"

Ellie said. "Now, come on…group hug!" Ellie muscled them together for an embrace, which Candy enjoyed, letting the close feeling soak in. She needed support for the afternoon ahead.

Maybe the team-leader issue would come up in a natural way, assuming they managed to stay in business mode, and they could talk about Candy becoming one.

"I've got to go," she said, breaking away reluctantly.

"Wait," Sara said. "Let's see where we stand on points before you leave." Sara fetched the chart she'd printed out and held it out for them to look at. "Our biggest competition is that team from Santa Monica, those cheaters. We have to outwit them somehow."

They went over upcoming events, including several at the *Sin on the Beach* party that night that she and Matt had agreed to participate in. When they were finished, Candy grabbed her purse and turned back to her friends. "Do I look businesslike enough?"

"Oh, definitely," Sara said.

"You look like a woman in love," Ellie said.

Candy opened her mouth to object, but Sara held up a hand. "She's not going to let it go, Candy. Just accept it."

"I guess so." Candy slid to the mirror in the entryway just to check. She looked…funny. Her face had too much color, even for the sunburn she'd accumulated, and her eyes were too bright. She looked like she had a fever.

Or like a woman in love.

"Hi, there." Matt stood on the other side of the screen door and her heart surged at the sight of him.

"Hi," she said.

"You look incredible," he said softly.

"Thank you," she said, so happy to have his eyes on her in that intense way Matt had.

"You ready to go?"

She nodded. "See you guys!" she called to her friends.

"Hold it!" Ellie said. "We have to see how Matt looks."

"God," Matt said, rolling his eyes. "Is there any point in refusing?"

"You know Ellie."

"I do." He sighed.

"Ready for the catwalk?" she asked.

"With you by my side, I can handle it." He grinned and extended his arm for her to grab. They were comrades in the coming ordeal and she loved that feeling. No matter what happened, they would be friends from here on. No more awkward tension about the Thong Incident, no more blushing and stammering when they ran into each other at Dark Gothic Roast.

They were friends now. Surely that made it worthwhile.

"Do a turn," Ellie commanded Matt.

"Lord," he said, looking sheepish under the scrutiny of three sets of female eyes. He took a slow turn in the summer weight Joseph Abboud suit that emphasized his height and build.

"What do you think?" Candy said, running her finger along the lapel. "I was going for a look that's tradi-tional, but still trendy. We bought him a blazer, too, so he can mix it up."

"Aren't we about to be late?" Matt asked, shooting his cuff to check his watch.

"The shirt is gorgeous," Ellie said. "And I love the tie."

"I know," Candy said. The shirt was a dense cotton

in antique white, the tie a high-end gray-blue stripe, restrained and elegant.

"And the haircut…" Ellie sighed. "Looks fabulous." She fingered his hair. "You could use some gel, I think."

"Forget the gel," Matt said, moving away. "Enough with the fashion show. Let's go." He took Candy by the elbow and led her out the door. She wiggled her fingers good-bye at her friends. "Wish us luck," she said. She had a feeling she'd need it.

An hour's drive later, they found the luncheon ballroom festive with flowers in honor of the theme— Planting the Seeds of Women's Leadership. Each seat held a small terra-cotta pot with a packet of seeds.

After they'd filled out name tags, Matt started toward the ballroom, no doubt to find a seat.

"Hang on. This is prime networking time." She caught his arm. "Let's talk strategy."

"There's a strategy?"

"Absolutely. Don't forget our card-gathering contest. Before we settle on a table, we circulate and collect cards. You go that way, I'll go the other and we'll meet in the middle. Then we'll sit with the strongest leads— where a longer conversation might net sales."

"Ah. I see. There is a strategy." He smiled at her, then surveyed the crowd of mostly women. "Looks like I'm seriously outnumbered."

"Use that to your advantage," she said, pressing his arm for emphasis. "You look very hot."

"You're suggesting I work it?" He raised a brow.

"If it makes a sale for SyncUp."

"I didn't realize you were so mercenary, Calder." He looked her over. "A hot mercenary, at least. Since you agreed to go to the convention with me, what's the winner of our little contest earn, anyway?"

"We should decide that, huh? Hmm. How about we do what Magellan suggested—have our own game of Truth or Bare? The winner asks a question the loser must answer." She would ask about the marketing teams. Perfect. Her heart raced.

Matt leaned down to talk near her ear. "Forget the Truth. Let's just go for Bare. That way we both win."

She trembled in response, aware that no matter how business-focused she managed to be, Matt could fell her with a word. The smell of him made her knees buckle and his kiss melted her bones altogether.

"Go get cards," she said, gently pushing him away from her. She moved in the opposite direction and paused at a group of women, determined to do her job.

Every time she looked up, though, Matt caught her eye, and it gave her such a rush. It was as if the ballroom smeared into the background so that all she saw was him. She ached to be alone with him again. They had something better to do than any one of the three-hundred people in this huge ballroom. It was their sweet secret.

Before long, they'd managed to work their way back to each other. Matt smiled at her as if to say, *at last*.

"How'd you do?" she asked him.

He fanned business cards like a poker hand, showing them to her in a way no one else would notice.

"Excellent," she said, then turned to introduce him

to the women she'd been chatting with. "I've been talking about Ledger Lite Personal, Matt. Sylvia thinks it would be a great idea."

Matt turned to Sylvia. "I'm glad to hear that..." Candy was pleased to see him use the techniques she'd taught him while he talked with the woman about her needs as a real-estate broker.

All of a sudden, Candy was being yanked into the perfumed arms of a woman who was hugging her. "Candy Calder, am I glad to see you."

She pulled back and recognized Claudia Stern, a woman who owned a mail-order infant-wear company. Candy had met her at a luncheon months ago. "You still with that computer firm, are you?" The woman hardly paused when Candy nodded. "Because I was wondering if you could squeeze in some freelance work. A bunch of us start-ups want to pool our cash and buy some ads and such. We're all knees and elbows and where-whichever about it, and I bragged I knew people and here you are—people!"

"I wish I could help, Claudia, but SyncUp keeps me pretty busy. I'm not doing any freelance work."

"Well, damn. That's a drag. Could you refer us to someone? Could you do that for us?"

"I'd be happy to. I'm sure I can suggest someone." They exchanged cards and Claudia pointed Candy's SyncUp card at her. "You call me now. I'm counting on you! We all are!"

"Did that woman just try to poach you from us?" Matt asked.

"I'm happy where I am," she said, then hesitated, realizing this was the perfect lead-in. "But now that you mention it, I did want to talk to you about ways I could be most useful to SyncUp. I'm ready for a new challenge and I was thinking that—"

"Matt? Is that you?"

They both turned to find a tall, sleek blonde smiling in surprised delight at Matt.

"Jane?" Matt said. "What are you doing here?"

This was Matt's Jane? She reminded Candy of the young Kathleen Turner. In a tailored pin-striped suit, pink silk blouse and subtle jewelry, with her hair in a soft braided twist, she was the picture of classic elegance.

"More importantly, Matt, what are *you* doing here? This is a *women's* luncheon," Jane said, in the same whiskey voice Turner was known for. The woman was direct and sexy as hell.

Matt turned to Candy, then to Jane, flummoxed about what to say, she could tell. "Jane Roston, I'd like you to meet a colleague of mine, Candy Calder, who brought me here."

"Nice to meet you," Jane said, but her gaze returned immediately to Matt. "You look great, Matt. All tanned. Great suit. Good haircut and…contacts? Are you wearing lenses?"

"Candy helped me update my look."

"Oh?" Her eyebrows went up and she looked Candy over, trying to figure out what was what.

"For work, of course," Candy said quickly. If Jane knew about the vacation fling, it might wreck the reconciliation, which Candy was counting on. That and the return of Serious Matt when they got back to L.A. The idea of getting this out of their system before the vacation ended had begun to seem impossible.

"Scott wants me to get better at networking and Candy's great at it, so she thought this luncheon would be a good place to work on my skills." He gave a short laugh.

"I see. That makes sense, I guess." She looked him over, a little puzzled. "So where'd the tan come from?"

"That. Oh. I'm at the beach. It was use it or lose it on my vacation days, so Ellie got me a place in Malibu."

"Me, too," Candy jumped in, then realized how that sounded. "Ellie's a friend and she and I and another friend are in a beach house, too. Except I'm working, too. And by coincidence, so was Matt, so it was natural for us to get together. To *work*. Together." *Shut up, Candy. Shut up.*

"Sure," Jane said slowly. "I guess."

Candy's stomach churned. Silence swelled while they all avoided each other's eyes. Her supposedly expert social skills seemed to have evaporated completely.

"What about you?" Matt asked Jane, finally saving them. "Why are you here?"

"Me? Oh. Our firm's being honored." She spoke slowly, as if still distracted by what was going on between Candy and Matt. "We did pro bono incorporations for some businesses and the partners needed a female to accept the plaque. I drew the short straw." She seemed to catch herself. "Not that this isn't a wonderful organization or anything, just that I'm swamped." She laughed, shaking her head, eyes wide, as if her work was stacked a mile high, but she loved it.

"As always, eh?" Matt smiled. "Jane's very dedicated."

"And what about you?" she said, pretending to be wounded. "You're at a business lunch in the middle of your vacation!"

This was a hot button for the couple, so Candy wanted to help. "But I had to drag Matt here. He's been in party mode for the entire trip."

"Party mode? Matt?" Jane tilted her head, quirking an eyebrow at him. "How have you been partying exactly?"

"Oh, with this and that," Matt said, clearing his throat, glancing at Candy.

"What hasn't he done? Karaoke…a limbo contest… beach volleyball…parasailing. I've been trying to get him to work with me on a project, but the man won't stop playing."

"Karaoke?" Jane's eyes widened. "You sang in public? I can't imagine." She laughed and leaned into him.

"Neither could I, but there was alcohol involved."

"That explains it. So what did you sing?"

"Something from *Grease*."

"You're the One that I Want." Candy remembered how fun it had been to sing with him, almost magical, and how the kiss had made it seem they'd meant every word of that song.

"A musical? I can't imagine," Jane said. "I'd give anything to have seen that. Just the thought makes me smile."

Matt laughed and Jane joined in, their bodies turned close.

"I'm sorry now I never asked you to take that ballroom dance class." She gave him a look of warm affection. "Tell you what. You can make it up to me by coming with me to a bar association dinner I have to attend. New-officer installation. I'll even rent your tux."

"I don't know, Jane." Matt looked completely flustered.

"I know it's tedious, but you'd be helping me out and you can tell me all about your fun vacation. Come on. You'll wow everyone." She looked him over appreciatively, then turned to Candy. "Good job on the new look."

"Thanks. Since Matt's a new VP, I thought he needed some…some…"

"Verve," Matt filled in for her.

"Verve?" Jane said. "My my, Matt. You *have* changed." She softened suddenly. "Anyway, you look wonderful. I love the contacts. I always said you had great eyes. Doesn't he have great eyes?" she asked Candy.

"Like Greg Kinnear," Candy said. "Or Kiefer Sutherland or…I mean…because his eyes are a strong feature, they needed emphasis." Her words went soft at the end. This conversation made her really uncomfortable.

"So here we are together at the same luncheon," Jane said, giving Matt a meaningful look. "It's a small world, huh?"

"Evidently," Matt said.

"Very small," Jane said, holding his gaze.

Candy had to get out of here and fast. She was definitely feeling like a third wheel on this bicycle. "I'll let you two catch up," she said. "Looks like they're seating people." She started away toward the tables.

"We can all sit together," Matt called to her.

"No, no. I'm fine." She grinned inanely, her heart a ball of agony in her chest. They looked so good standing there together. Jane was tall enough to look Matt eye-to-eye, whereas Candy was way too short for him.

Of course that wasn't what mattered in a couple—whether or not their heights matched. What mattered was what they had in common, which, for Matt and Jane, was just about everything, she'd bet. Candy could picture them Sunday mornings, laptops side-by-side, catching up on e-mail on their pillow-lush canopy bed in some fabulous suburban McMansion.

Not that she had anything against big houses or fancy beds. Her brothers and parents were well-off and she wanted that, too. She was being childishly jealous, mostly of the familiarity between Matt and Jane—the shared jokes, the old teases, the long history, the affection.

She wanted that. A history with someone. Spending all this time with Matt had showed her that. She vowed right now to find some fun-loving guy who wanted to settle in with her in a way that was comfortable, but still lively. Stable, but full of surprises. Someone she could count on, someone strong enough to handle the occasional shakeup. Yeah.

She took a seat at a faraway table full of chatting women, but she couldn't help glancing at Matt and Jane, engrossed in conversation, laughing together, leaning in to each other.

This was excellent in the long run. Really. An extra bonus. Her makeover had been so successful that Matt's ex-girlfriend wanted him back. Candy was *good*. Just as Matt had said.

She swallowed down her envy, ignored the hollow feeling inside and introduced herself to the woman next to her. She would talk about Ledger Lite Personal, dammit. She could work as hard as she played. Even when her heart was a fist-sized lump rattling in her empty, aching chest. No way would she lock herself into a stall in the ladies' room and bawl her eyes out.

MATT HELD JANE'S CHAIR for her, but he kept his eye on Candy, who seemed to be doing fine. She'd said something to make the woman next to her laugh. Two other women were leaning across the table to get in on the fun, too. She was okay.

Candy could handle herself. She'd smoothed over his fumbling remarks when they ran into Jane, making what they were doing sound perfectly reasonable, then left him with Jane. She probably saw it as a good deed.

She'd left emotionally, too. Slipped away, quick as a darting fish he couldn't quite catch, no matter how close it seemed or how tight his fingers gripped it. A shiver and it zipped out of reach.

"You can sit now, Matt," Jane said, smiling back at him where he stood watching Candy.

"Oh, uh, yeah," he said, then sat beside her.

Jane had accepted the idea of him and Candy working together on vacation. Hell, she'd asked him to dinner right in front of Candy.

In fact, Candy, no doubt, believed they were getting back together this very moment. If he wanted to end the affair with her, this would do the trick. He remembered what Magellan had said, that he'd let Candy believe a falsehood for her own good. Here was his chance to make the lie stick.

Except what had Mr. All Knowing added? *The truth shall set you free.* Maybe so. He certainly had no interest in lying. Not to Candy. Not to Jane. And not to himself.

Their table mates were all talking and Jane bent close, speaking intimately to him. "I like the new you, Matt. A lot."

"So I guess I no longer need fun to throw me a surprise party?"

Jane grimaced. "That was out of line, I know. If it makes you feel better, my therapist suggested I apologize. I am sorry, Matt. I blamed you for my own frustration, my own ennui. I made you the symbol of my being stuck."

He fought the urge to roll his eyes at the psychobabble. "You had a point, though. I have been working too hard. This vacation has opened my eyes."

"That's good. Very good." She studied him. "Sometimes a breather is all people need. A fresh perspective." She held his gaze, offering him another chance.

They could go back to how they'd been—carefully planned weekend excursions, evenings that didn't interfere with work. Sex in its place. Sex with Jane had been perfectly fine.

But it hadn't been wild or unpredictable or overwhelming. It hadn't left him breathless and aching, as with Candy.

It also wouldn't leave him heartbroken, angry and devastated, which, he'd bet, was how things would end with Candy.

Jane shared his values. She fit his formula. She would be a fine life companion, a comfortable habit.

But love was more than a routine you got into. Candy was right about that. She'd made him want more.

The debate was irrelevant, really. If Jane had been the most scintillating woman in the world—his soul mate, if that was possible—it wouldn't have changed a thing.

He was in love with Candy. Whether she offered a comfortable routine or an uncontrollable roller coaster, she was the woman he loved. There was no room for anyone else.

He'd lost his heart to a woman he couldn't possibly have.

There was nothing to be done about that now, except he had to clear the air with Jane. A straight line to the truth was best. "You were right to break up with me, Jane. I think we're too much alike to be good for each other."

Her face stilled. She was startled by his words, but she managed a gracious smile. "But that's a positive indicator, don't you think? Being alike?"

"Not if you end up in a rut together."

She studied him. "We had some inertia to deal with, but…"

"Maybe we both needed to get shaken up a bit."

"You don't want to try again then?" Anger and hurt were sharp undertones to her flat question.

He shook his head, then put his hand over hers. "You're a wonderful person, Jane, and I wish you the very best. You deserve a guy who'll ballroom dance with you, not one you have to drag from his computer for a movie."

Jane's lip trembled and her eyes filled. He would hug her, but he knew she would hate that. Jane had a lot of dignity. He sat with her, holding her hand, waiting to see what she needed to do—yell at him, insult him, even throw water in his face.

But abruptly, she seemed to get control. Her eyes cleared, her shoulders dropped and she managed a quick smile. "You're not one to soften the blow, are you? No easing into it for Matt Rockwell." She shook her head, as if she was laughing at herself. "Actually, I always liked that about you."

She took her hand from him, adjusted her napkin, drank some water and, when she looked back at him, she was completely composed. "You're right, of course," she said steadily. "I knew we were never on fire for each other. And I want that. I do."

"You deserve that."

Her smile twisted. "It's no fun to be alone. Seeing you here, I thought maybe we had enough to make it work. But we would be…settling. That's true." Her lip wobbled again and she reached for her water.

To give her space, Matt looked away. His gaze snagged on Candy and held.

When he looked back at Jane, she'd followed his line of sight. "You're worried about her? She's chattering away just fine. We have a paralegal like that. Never stops talking." She made her hand into a yakking puppet. "Terminally bubbly."

Anger spiked at her easy dismissal of Candy. Too many people mistook her surface liveliness for superficiality. "People underestimate Candy. She's smart and funny—and wise, too. You have to give her time to show you."

Jane took in a sharp breath. Her face changed, went

still and cold, as if sheeted in ice. "Ah. I see." She fiddled angrily with a tablespoon, making it clunk again and again against the linen cloth. "I don't get it, but I see. So, she makes you happy? Is that it? Keeps you out of a rut?" Her voice cracked.

"She and I work together, Jane. It's impossible." And it wasn't only work. Candy would exhaust, annoy and eventually infuriate him. Sooner rather than later. And once Fun Guy packed up his vacation duffel, the old Matt would bore the hell out of Candy. They were a dead end for certain.

"Whatever," Jane said dismissively. She grabbed a roll and buttered it, fiercely at first. Her movements slowed, she set down her butter knife with a click and looked at him. "It doesn't matter, I know. You and I are done. If you find someone else, good for you." She looked over at Candy, again, as if the possibility of Matt and Candy puzzled her.

"Candy and I work together. We couldn't ever—"

"Whatever!" She cut one hand in a stop-arguing gesture, then sighed. "If it weren't for these damnable social events, I wouldn't mind being alone at all."

"I understand." He was impressed with her ability to rise above her emotions, to analyze and conquer them so smoothly. "Listen, Jane. About the bar dinner. I'd be honored to accompany you. And I'll pay for the tux myself."

"If I don't snag a date, I might take you up on that. I've got feelers out, though, so no worries. I don't waste time." She grabbed his hand. "You're a good person, Matt. In my nobler moments, I want the best for you, too."

They smiled at each other. He realized they'd broken up for good with no fuss at all. He felt relieved and he was sure Jane did, too.

What did it say about him that he could be involved with a woman for nearly a year without any more angst than a mild argument? Come to think of it, he'd always avoided strong feelings. His relationship with Heather had been an anomaly.

Was it because of how devastated his mother had been when their father left? She'd always been highly strung and vulnerable, but after that she seemed to crumble. Matt had had to be strong for her and Ellie.

Those terrible first months he'd handled the tasks that befuddled his mother—the wonky thermostat, the failing Pathfinder, the bills that piled up. She'd slept so much that Matt cooked meals, got groceries, cared for Ellie—quizzed her on spelling words, made sure she brushed her teeth and bathed. He'd read her bedtime stories and reassured her when she stood outside their mother's locked door, needing a mother's comfort.

It was then that he'd strengthened the habit of controlling his emotions, of keeping his head down to focus on the task at hand. He'd valued what made sense and avoided what didn't—like the human heart.

His mother never really returned to normal, although she managed to make ends meet with a bookkeeping job, which meant he'd remained watchful and careful, slow to get involved, always holding back.

It wasn't just the trauma of his father's departure, though. It was how he was. It had felt right to be that way. As he'd told Candy, that was how he was wired.

But now he'd met Candy and his barriers were dissolving, his natural need for distance melting away. This alarmed him, but he was a realist and couldn't ignore it.

Should he talk to Candy? Take this chance? But how could he? The situation seemed impossible. Even if he wasn't her boss, they were as different as he and Jane were alike.

What should he do? He felt twisted into knots, his head ready to burst, his lungs so tight every breath burned. He felt as though he'd been slammed by a huge wave, tossed into a cloud of sand and sea until he didn't know which direction to swim for air. If this was love, maybe he was better off without it.

13

KNOWING IT WOULD BE a mistake, Candy stole a glance at the table where Matt and Jane sat. Sure enough, Jane was leaning in to speak in Matt's ear. His arm was across the back of her chair and he seemed completely at ease with her.

An old, old song started up in Candy's head. *Smile, though your heart is breaking.* The lyrics promised that if you did that—smiled through heartbreak—the sun would shine through.

Yeah, right. She felt like a big old rain cloud about to unload fat drops all over the linen cloth.

This was why she never got serious with anyone. This terrible hole in her heart. This bottomless ache. She'd been smart enough to avoid it for twenty-nine years. Maybe being so indulged as a child meant she'd had no practice in disappointment, but she'd stayed clear of it anyway. She didn't need to touch the red coil to know the stove would burn her.

This was good, what had happened. Matt and Jane were back together—they even had a date. And all thanks to Candy. She'd done the right thing. She should be proud.

Except she felt utterly bereft. It was so like her to get

hooked on someone she couldn't have—and didn't really want. She wanted it all, spoiled child that she was. As with Brad, she wanted him to ask her to marry him, even though she'd have said no. She was doing it again, dammit.

Just when she feared she'd embarrass herself by bursting into tears in the middle of the conversation, the dessert mousse arrived and the program commenced, giving her time to regroup, listen and soothe herself with chocolate.

No point bitching about the pain. Suck it up and move on. Jane's appearance was fate's tap on the shoulder. *Hey, you. Remember who you are and why you're here.*

She did. She remembered. And she would push forward. She'd go back to her place, finalize the marketing plan and when Matt praised her, she'd bring up the promotion. It was time. She'd fulfilled her side of their deal—given Matt a makeover, taught him networking, even repaired his love life.

Talk about a bonus! She always went the extra mile. Wasn't that what team leaders did?

Right.

The good news was that now that Matt and Jane had reconciled, Candy had no more worries about how she and Matt would end this. It was over and done.

Her plan in place, Candy found the program interminable. There seemed to be an honoree at every table. By the time the stack of plaques was down to a few, she'd eaten two untouched desserts and had three decaf refills.

Jane was as classy in her acceptance remarks as she'd

seemed when Candy met her. Candy kept her eyes trained away from where Matt sat—no doubt watching Jane—afraid if she caught his adoring expression, she'd burst into jealous tears.

Eventually the last polite applause filled the room. Finally released, Candy barreled for the doors instead of pausing to reinforce her rapport with potential clients as she would normally do in networking mode. She'd grabbed plenty of cards before disaster struck. She managed to catch Matt's eye and pointed toward the parking lot, so he'd meet her at the car.

Grateful to be outside, she sucked in smoggy air and fought the tumult inside. *Get a grip. He was never yours.* They'd had an affair. *Don't cling. Let go.* She only wished she'd known their final lovemaking had been the last, so she could have memorized every touch. It was like wolfing down the last Cheeto before you realized the bag was empty. You wanted to savor the final lovely morsel.

The good news, though, was that she was anxious to get back to work. She'd learned that much about herself. She could work when it mattered. She was not *just* a party girl.

She watched Matt wend his way to their car, his expression anxious. When he reached her, he asked, "Are you ill? I saw you run out."

"Just anxious to go," she said with a fake smile, ducking into the car to avoid him.

Matt sat in the driver's seat. "There was room at the table," he said softly. "I didn't mean for you to leave."

"It was much better, Matt, and you know it. Jane liked the new you, which is great. Isn't it?" He seemed too quiet.

"Nothing changed between Jane and me," he said after a pause. He sounded weary and troubled. Maybe out of guilt?

"Give it time," she said, glancing at him. "You got a start at it. I probably cramped your style."

"It's not like that, Candy. It won't ever be." He hesitated, as though he had something more to say, then looked out the windshield.

"Let's head back," she said, nodding forward. "I want to finish my marketing plan so I can show it to you."

She felt him staring at her. "We need to talk."

"There's nothing to say, Matt. I get it."

"No, you don't. That's the point. We—"

"Let's just *go!*" she said with clenched teeth, wringing the burgundy napkin that in her haste she'd taken with her. She'd twisted it so tightly it hurt her fingers. Unshed tears made her nose burn.

"We need to talk about us, about what we're going to do."

His cell phone rang, interrupting him. He fumbled for it, reading the display. "Scott," he muttered.

"Take it," she said, grateful for the reprieve.

"Hi, Scott. What's up?" Matt said tightly. "Yeah? Where are we on the reorg? Uh…" He paused, glanced at her, then out the side window. He couldn't talk to Scott freely with her in the car. "Not too far." He cleared his throat. "I'm on vacation, remember? Use it or lose it?" he said in a falsely hearty voice. He paused, listening, then spoke again, his tone serious.

"I'll get on that…um, plan…when I get back…. Sunday? Not Sunday. Sunday's a day of rest." He laughed. "Be careful what you wish for, Scott. I'm addressing my PQ2 weaknesses, which means I'm taking it easier. I won't be in the office 24-7 anymore."

He winked at Candy, telling her he'd learned from her. "Unintended consequences, I guess." He looked at her again, his expression full of gratitude and affection. Then she saw an idea dawn on him. He held up a finger to her.

"Scott, one thing. What do you think about a consumer version of Ledger Lite? We'd market it to our Paycheck Plus customers?" He listened, then turned to nod at her, indicating Scott's interest.

"It's Candy Calder's idea," he said quickly. "I was talking to her and—" He stopped cold. "Uh—before I left. We ran into each other…" He swallowed hard, panicked and jerked his gaze out front again. It must have dawned on him he didn't dare let Scott know they were together on vacation.

"So, she's, uh, putting together a plan…. Sure, sure… I'll tell her—when I get back, of course. At the next meeting." His face was bright red and he sounded guilty as hell.

Matt put away his phone and rubbed the back of his neck. "That was weird. I almost blew it. Sorry I lied."

"You had to, Matt. If Scott knew we were together, it would be utterly weird." And there was no way Matt could comfortably keep the secret back at SyncUp. If he gave her the promotion, everyone would think she slept her way there. "I appreciate you talking up my idea to Scott. It means a lot." Again, her throat closed.

"It's the least I could do. After all you've done for

me." He stopped. "You know I mean the lessons, not the...not us together. And I would have told him anyway. It's a great idea."

"I know that," she said softly, realizing how the sex had muddied everything between them. Matt was having trouble figuring out his own motivations. "I was glad to hear you say you wouldn't be working so hard from now on."

"You helped me figure that out," he said, turning to her. "There's something else I need to say. And it's not about work. Being with you has meant so much to me. *You* mean so much to me."

"You mean a lot to me, too, Matt. But that's beside the point. You have Jane. We have work."

"Jane and I are done, Candy. Period."

"We had a deal. We have to stick with it."

"We need to talk about us."

"There *is* no us, Matt!" She didn't mean to raise her voice, but he'd just thrown away her garlic—Jane—and her heart was racing with pointless hope. "You could hardly manage a lie to Scott about me. We have to quit while we're ahead."

He studied her. "Is that what you want?"

"It's what we both want." When she tried to smile, her lips trembled like a muscle held too long.

They sat in silence for a few beats, both staring out the windshield. "Okay. If that's it, then," Matt said finally, starting the car with tense, almost-angry movements.

After they'd driven for a while in awkward silence, she thought of something to get them on track. "So how many cards did you get, by the way?" she asked softly.

"I don't know. You count." He fished out his wallet and handed it to her.

She counted them. "Twelve! That's excellent." It was so hard to sound cheerful when she was so miserable. "I got twenty, so, at two-to-one, you beat me by four cards. Congratulations. You won." Her smile felt glued onto her cardboard face. "So you can ask me any question you like. That's your prize."

"I don't know, Candy," he said, sounding discouraged.

"Think about it. Drop me off at my place, I'll grab the computer and meet you at yours to show you my marketing plan. You can ask me the question when I get there."

They didn't talk the rest of the way and she was glad. She ached as if she'd been everyone's target in a dodgeball game where they used rocks instead of balls.

She would push past this, though. She had to. This was what she'd worked for. She couldn't give up when she was so close.

UNLOCKING HIS BEACH house, Matt caught his reflection in the glass of the storm door. He hardly recognized the *GQ* guy staring back at him with the fancy haircut and pricey shades. Fun Guy. Who'd just been shot down by the woman he loved.

She was right. Being together at SyncUp would be difficult, to say the least. She wanted it to be over. She was sticking with their deal. Maybe that's what he should do.

Accept her decision, let it go. He loved her, but he'd get over it. Maybe she loved him, too, but not enough to try to work it out. Should he push her? Why? Why make her spell out all the reasons why he was wrong for her? All that BS about oil and water and oranges? Why put himself through that misery?

He stood on his porch and looked out at the ocean.

He noticed a parachute, bright against the blue sky, skimming by. A parasailor. He remembered Candy up in the air, the way she'd been terrified, but pushed past it. *Don't you dare,* she'd said, eyes flashing, when he wanted to call it off. *I want to try this.*

He had to try, too—go for it the way Candy had. Push through the fear, take the risk—no matter what she said to him. If she loved him, they would figure out how to be together. He saluted that faraway parasailor, then stepped off the porch, headed for Candy, come what may.

CANDY SHOVED MATT'S computer in its case and started out, not even stopping to change clothes. She'd kicked off her shoes and removed her pantyhose to cross the beach in comfort at least. She didn't dare stop moving or her feelings would hit and she'd dissolve into a heap of heartbreak.

This was more than a vacation fling with Matt. She had feelings for him that weren't going away as ordered. She was trapped and the misery would hit as soon as she held still long enough to feel it.

It reminded her of stubbing her toe and the seconds of nothing before the pain struck, when she had time to brace for it, guessing how bad it would be this time.

When she looked toward Matt's place, she noticed he was headed her way, taking long, purposeful strides, his expression fixed with determination.

About what? About her? About them? Against all

reason, hope made her heart sing and she started to run toward him.

Seeing her, Matt also ran, then stopped when they were close. He was breathing hard and she was, too.

"I've got my question." He paused. "Forget Sync-Up, forget our deal and tell me the truth—how do you feel about me?"

"How do I feel…?" She swallowed hard, not sure what she should say, fighting dizziness, struggling to be sensible.

"Let me make it simpler. I'm in love with you, Candy."

"You are? In love? With me?" Her heart was doing a fluttering hip-hop. She needed to sit down. Fast.

Sensing her faintness, he caught her by her elbows. "I am. So, what about you? Do you feel the same?"

"Do I?" Her mind was as fuzzy as a radio off its station. "I mean, yes, I do… I love you." She said it with wonder, surprised to hear the words come out of her mouth.

At the same time, she knew in her soul they were true.

"That's good, then," he said. "We feel the same." He leaned in to kiss her, but she held back.

"No, that's bad. What about SyncUp?"

"We'll work it out…somehow." His words faded and she knew he'd gone fuzzy, too, unwilling to address the impossibility of a future between them. "For now, let's just be here. Together."

"Okay," she answered automatically. This solution erased the agony she'd anticipated with so much dread. Matt was a smart guy. If he thought they could figure it out, maybe they could. She let her doubts melt away. She let her love for Matt take charge, pushing away

SyncUp, even her promotion. They would discuss that soon enough. That would be part of working things out.

She knew this was wrong thinking on her part, but right now she was glad to escape the pain, to have more time in Matt's arms. They hurried to his place. She set his computer on the table and they stumbled to his bed, pulling off each other's clothes, laughing, breathless and amazed.

Could she really have this? Be in love with Matt? Despite their differences, despite work—

Stop! She wouldn't think about that. It would ruin the moment and right now Matt was looking at her naked body *that way* again, like no other man, as though every inch of her was worth a lifetime of study, as though being able to touch her was a gift beyond measure.

She wanted this. So much.

"I can't believe I have you in my bed," Matt said, his eyes a hot blue that promised his love and all the support she could ever want.

"Believe it. I'm here." At the same time she felt a tension inside, a held breath, the sense there was trouble ahead, that this wasn't quite real.

Matt kissed her then, deeply, his tongue searching her mouth, while one hand slid down her body to her thighs and stroked her neediest place.

She parted her legs, inviting him inside, welcoming the rush of pleasure they'd felt together before.

Matt pushed into her, holding her gaze, and the moment was different, more serious. This was for keeps. "When I'm inside you, I never want to leave."

"Then don't," she said, crossing her heels over his back, wrapping her arms around his shoulders.

He kissed her hungrily, as if she were the source of his strength. They held each other so tight their bodies seemed melded together. Only their hips parted long enough to make short strokes. They were so in tune with each other that the tiniest movement from Matt sent spirals of pleasure through her. She could tell she had the same effect on him. Sex had never been so powerful or so intimate for her.

She felt her orgasm gather and sensed his doing the same.

"I don't want to come yet," she said.

"There's plenty more after this," he breathed, quickening his pace, moving in a way she couldn't resist. "Just let go."

Her climax began, then seemed to move to Matt, as if they shared the sensation, and he sent it back to her even stronger than before. Waves of pleasure poured through her, so strong she had tears in her eyes. Matt's face was full of emotion, too.

Slowly, the intensity lessened and she became aware of the beat of Matt's heart, in time with hers, heard the matched rhythm of their breathing. She never imagined feeling this close to another person. She knew that, no matter what happened, this was worth it.

She closed her eyes and held on to Matt.

They made love for what seemed like a long time and yet only moments. Rolling over after one more amazing orgasm, Candy caught sight of Matt's travel clock. "God! It's six, Matt. We have to get dressed for the beach party."

"I've got a party right here. Come as you are." He nuzzled her neck, finding her with his fingers.

She pushed his hand away with a reluctant groan. "I promised Ellie and Sara we'd do the events." She struggled out of bed and bent to drag on her clothes. "I've got to go shower and change at my place."

"You're serious about this?" Matt said, watching her.

"One of us has to be." She leaned down to kiss his sweet mouth. "And now that you're Fun Guy, I guess it's me."

"I know," he said, flopping back against the pillow, hands under his head, elbows out. "I don't think I'll ever be the same." He looked deliciously strong, tanned and relaxed, the sheet bunched at his waist, sexier than ever. Of course she was seeing him through the eyes of love.

Grabbing up Sara's blazer, she noticed Matt's computer, where she'd practically thrown it on the table. She had to show him the marketing plan, talk about the teams, but when?

Maybe tomorrow? Or the next day? Before they left Malibu anyway. When they were ready to deal with the logistics of continuing an affair back at SyncUp. Because they had to continue this.

She and Matt were in love. She couldn't quite believe it. Or sort it out or figure out how it would work. For now, just knowing was enough. It had to be.

MATT GOT READY while Candy went to her place to change. After his shower, he scrubbed some of that ridiculous gel into his hair and put on the Hawaiian shirt Candy liked. He had to change shorts twice to get the right match. Now he was getting vain?

This was all pretty crazy. He'd promised Candy they

would work it out, but he wasn't sure how. A vague tension anchored itself in his gut, but he wasn't going to deal with it yet. He wanted to float a while longer on the cloud he'd been on since Candy and he had wrestled her phone away from Radar.

He headed out to get her, enjoying the breeze, the sleek gray sheen of the ocean laid out before him, the waves rolling like the shivering pelt of a huge slow-moving beast.

The neon of the carnival rides glowed against the sunset sky. Down the beach, there were bonfires and he could hear the gathering noise of a crowd. Music, too. He and Candy could dance.

He wanted to dance? Unbelievable. But he realized if Candy wanted him to, he'd freak dance in front of God and everyone. He was in love. The way he'd been with Heather, all those years ago, except now he was mature enough to handle the roller coaster.

At least he hoped he was.

His gut tightened again.

Until he caught sight of Candy heading his way. The sight of her erased all his doubts. She'd changed how he saw everything.

She wore a strapless dress that exposed her shoulders and the tops of her breasts. When she was close enough he noticed a diamond on a chain resting in the hollow of her throat. He wanted to kiss her there, in that tender place. And everywhere else, too.

She threw her arms around him and he picked her up and spun her around, kissing her as he set her back down on the sand.

"Sorry I'm late," she said, looking up at him, her eyes full of love. "Sara had to know why I looked feverish, so I explained that I'm crazy in love."

"So I make you feverish? All hot…and achy? You do that to me, too."

"Mm-hmm," she said. "I told her we were working everything out at SyncUp. Do you think we can?" She bit her pretty lip.

"Of course." He kissed away the bite mark, feeling the familiar wash of heat and need whenever he touched her. She melted into his arms again.

"You sure about this party?"

"I promised," she said on a groan.

"How about a quickie?" He nuzzled her neck, loving the way she softened against him, so willing, as eager for more as he was. "There's always time for a quickie."

"Later, Matt." She sighed. "It'll have to be later."

Every time they made love, his feelings grew stronger. Surely, that would be enough to get them through the troubles to come. Whenever he tried to think past this vacation, his brain shorted out. *Wait and see* was all he could come up with.

Weird. He wasn't a guy who waited for things to fall into place. He knew you made your own luck, but, for some reason, he was content to ride this out. A bad sign, but looking into Candy's sweet face, he refused to figure out exactly what this meant.

Inside the fence that marked off the *Sin on the Beach* party, he waited while Candy signed them up for some mortifying activity or other.

"Matt!"

He spun in time for Ellie to throw her arms around him. "Sara told me what happened. I'm so happy for you." She kissed his cheek. "I knew this would work out."

"So this was one of your setups? To get me and Candy together?" Not that he minded a bit now.

"I always knew you'd be good together."

"You never said anything to me."

"Would it have done any good?" She put her hands on her hips.

"No. But, I gotta say, I'm going to let you nose into my business more often if this is what results."

Ellie laughed, her eyes shiny with triumph. "I'm glad to hear it. Candy wasn't easy to convince, either. I had to twist her arm big-time. That Q-E-2 thingie—the personality test? Her results had her flipped out, but I convinced her that if she brought work here she could prove to you what a good team leader she'd make!"

"Team leader? What?" He stared at Ellie. "What do you know about the teams?"

"Just what Candy told me. That you have to appoint leaders to a bunch of teams and she wants to be one. Didn't you talk about that?" She hesitated. "Sara said you'd worked it all out, so I just assumed—"

"No one's supposed to know about the teams."

"Uh-oh. Yeah, that was a secret. I forgot. Someone told her anyway. Pretend I didn't say anything. She'll talk with you, I know. The point is she'll be great at it, right?"

"This is not good, Ellie." His head spun. Candy wanted to be a product manager? That explained her obsession with showing him Ledger Lite and going on about new challenges and her ideas. No wonder she sounded as though she were interviewing for a job half the time. She was.

The music swelled, irritatingly loud, and bonfire smoke burned his eyes, thanks to the contacts he wasn't used to yet.

"It'll be fine. Just talk to her." Ellie searched his face, worried, then seemed to notice someone approaching from behind him. "Here she comes. Don't let me ruin this, Matt."

He turned and saw that Candy held a margarita in each hand and wore a big grin.

This would be bad.

"You need to go, El," he said firmly. "I need to talk to Candy alone."

"Can I explain it to her at least?" She answered her own question. "No. You're right. But don't be blunt, for God's sake. For once use some diplomacy."

"I'll handle it," he said, making a shooing motion.

She turned and left before Candy reached him.

Candy held out a margarita. "Where's Ellie going?"

Matt shrugged off the question. "Let's find a quiet place." He put his arm around her shoulder, his gut aching.

"You bad boy. At a party...?" She glanced at her watch. "We do have a few minutes before the first event. There's a spot." She pointed at a cove where the embers of a fading campfire glowed red.

She thought he was after that quickie. If only. Dread filled him, cold and gray, but delaying the truth wouldn't help either of them.

When they reached the spot, Matt smoothed sand from a rock that would hold them both. They sat together and he placed his untouched margarita on the sand at their feet.

She sipped hers, then looked up at him. Her smile faltered. "What's wrong, Matt?"

There was no easy way to approach this, so he just said it. "Ellie mentioned that you want to be a product team leader."

"I…um… She told you?"

"She thought you and I had already discussed it. Something Sara said about us working things out. How did you hear about the teams anyway?"

"I overheard Daisy on the phone and—"

"Talked her into giving you the scoop?" He smiled, knowing how persuasive Candy could be. "So, this whole working vacation deal was about the promotion?"

"In a way." Candy grimaced, seeming embarrassed. "I knew you had a bad impression of me, so this was a chance to show you what I can do."

"I know what you can do, Candy. That's never been an issue. My problem is figuring out which team to put you on—where you and the team would benefit the most."

"You're putting me *on* a team, not in charge of one?"

He nodded. "The team leader job is mostly coordination and facilitation. Meetings, planning sessions. Stuff you'd hate."

"Do you like meetings and planning?" she asked sharply.

"No, but—"

"But you do them because you have to. So can I. The point is that you don't see me as a leader. Why not?" She was angry now, he could tell, and hurt.

"You'd be bored in a week, Candy. You wouldn't be using your strengths."

"And what are those?"

"Creativity, divergent thinking, innovation."

"I have other strengths. Leadership, for one thing. And I can do planning. My marketing plan references the strategic plan, for example, and if you'll look at it—"

"I'm sorry, Candy. I'll push your Ledger Lite idea with Scott, and I know you'll make a great contribution to whatever team I put you on, but—"

"You won't even consider me?" She looked utterly bereft. She blinked fast, fighting tears.

God, he'd made her cry. What a jerk. He had to fix this. "Maybe you have a preference for what team you want to work on? I can't promise, of course. That would be favoritism and we have to avoid that."

She stared at him, swallowed hard, made her hands into fists. She was shaking, too.

All he wanted to do was give her what she wanted somehow. "Would you prefer the financial products team? That's where Ledger Lite is. It's dialed in, though. Not much need for creativity, so I'm not sure you'd like that…"

He babbled on about the other teams, giving her details he shouldn't be sharing with an employee— anything to help her feel better about the situation.

"You never considered me. I can't believe it. And nothing I can show you will change that?"

"I know your talents, Candy. You didn't need to scheme with Ellie to show me."

"It wasn't a scheme. It was a demonstration." Now she

was getting angry. "It's because of my reputation, isn't it? Because everyone thinks I play around too much."

"Of course not." He stopped, realizing there was some truth to her point. "It is true that if you were to become a team leader, we'd have to deal with staff perceptions about you, but that's not the point. The point is—"

"And what are those perceptions? That I'm a party girl? That I'm not serious about work?"

"That's not the issue."

"The issue is that you don't respect me, Matt."

"Of course I respect you. I respect you too much to put you in a position where you can't shine. Why would you even want that?"

"Because I want to get ahead, dammit. I want to move to the next level. But you *respect* me too much to do that for me, right?" Her words dripped with sarcasm.

"I can't, Candy. It's not right for you or for SyncUp. I want to make you happy, believe me, I do. I love you."

"Then give me the job. That's what will make me happy. If you love—" She stopped herself, as if shocked at what she'd been about to say and what he'd actually suggested—giving her the job because he cared about her.

"That's exactly why you can't give it to me, isn't it? We're sleeping together. You can't promote me even if you wanted to. And you don't even want to." Her voice caught.

"Candy," he said softly, not liking her train of thought at all. "I can't give you a job that's not right for you. Our sleeping together has nothing to do with that."

She stared at him, her eyes full of accusation, her face full of anguish. "You're wrong, Matt," she said softly. "It has everything to do with it."

She stared at him and he felt the ground shift beneath his feet. They'd agreed not to think through the implications of their affair or of falling in love, but that had been foolish, he saw now. He hadn't been himself. He'd been lost in the fog of being Fun Guy. And that, he saw clearly for the first time, had been a big mistake. Somehow, he had to fix it for Candy. He had no right to drag her down because he'd been an irresponsible ass.

14

THEIR SLEEPING TOGETHER changed everything, Candy saw now. She felt as though she'd been yanked awake, blinking into the dark, her heart pounding, as hard reality replaced her soft and silly dreams.

She'd practically said it right out: *If you love me, give me the job.* How sick was that? Maybe at an unconscious level she *had* believed that having sex with Matt—getting closer to him, anyway—would ensure her promotion, or at least allow him to see her in a more positive light.

Even if she'd never had that awful idea, even if she had earned the promotion, how could Matt promote a lover, no matter how talented? It just wouldn't look right.

But that was a moot point, since he didn't consider her capable of the job. All her efforts to fix her reputation with him had failed.

This was all wrong, all terrible. She dug her nails into her palms to keep from crying. She didn't know which bad angle to examine first.

"Don't catastrophize, Candy. Our being together makes things complicated, but we can figure it out." She could see he was flailing for a solution, but his eyes told her he knew it was hopeless, too.

"How? Just because we want to keep the personal separate from the professional doesn't mean we can."

He looked at her, letting her words sink in.

"How could we behave normally at SyncUp? How could you evaluate my performance? You'd be too strict or too lenient, and I'd wonder which and why. And what would people think? They would find out, you know. It's inevitable. And I hate the idea of them gossiping about how we got together and why and what it means."

"We'll handle it," he said stubbornly, but she could see he was as troubled as she was. "Day by day."

"And when we break up? How will that be?"

"You expect us to break up?" Matt asked.

"People do. What makes us special? What do we have in common really? Sex and our taste in junk food. You said yourself, you need common goals and a routine to stay together. We'd drive each other crazy, disappoint each other over and over. Of course we'd break up." She stopped, feeling hysterical, crazed. So hurt and disappointed and scared she didn't know what to do.

"You're giving up before we've even started," he said. "Look, you're hurt about the team leader thing. Okay…" He swallowed hard, breathing raggedly. "What if I assigned *acting* managers. I could put together teams on a temporary basis. You could try it out and if it didn't work, no harm done. I'd make the permanent appointments and no one would be the wiser. I think I could sell that to Scott—"

"Stop it, Matt." She hated that he was trying to appease her this way. "You can't give me the job to soothe my feelings. You wouldn't do this for anyone else and you know it. Let's cut to the chase. Isn't that what you prefer? Our relationship is a mistake. It wrecks everything." She jumped to her feet.

He stood, too. "What are you saying?"

"That it's over. We're done. We should have stuck with the original deal. This is all wrong. I have to go. Tell Ellie and Sara I'm sorry, but I can't stay for the party." Her heart felt as if it might explode. She turned and began to run.

"Candy!" Matt called, but he didn't follow her and she was glad. Being with him had been a mistake. She'd been weak and stupid and now everything was so much worse.

She'd never had a chance at the promotion. That made her feel physically ill. Worse, she'd have to go back to SyncUp and work with Matt.

There were good reasons for those no-sex-in-the-workplace rules, all right. Every time she saw him, the pain would hit again. The pain and the disappointment.

How could she even stay at SyncUp, knowing Matt didn't take her seriously? Would the word get out that she'd been turned down? Would word get out about their affair? Would it show in their faces? How could she ever hold her head up again?

On top of all that, she was breaking up with the man she loved. This was pure agony. She had to escape somehow, stop the pain or delay it until she was in better shape or something.

"Hey, you're going the wrong way, lady." Carter called to her from a few yards away, Radar at his heels. "The party's in that direction." He pointed behind her.

"I'm not up for a party right now," she said. "I'm feeling too blue." The understatement of the century.

"Blue, huh? Then what you need is a martini to match your mood at WHIM SIM. Better yet, a bunch of us are playing darts for shots. You can be on my team."

"Darts, huh?" She liked darts. She liked Carter, too. He was the kind of fun-loving guy she always went for, back when she'd been content to be who she was, not struggling to get all serious and work-obsessed.

Radar whined up at her, but he sounded more anxious than eager for her to join them.

"Do you get festival points?" At least she could earn something for the competition to help her friends.

"Yeah, I guess. I think I saw that posted."

"Then let's go," she said. "We're wasting time and blue booze."

"Girl after my own heart." Carter slung a friendly arm around her shoulder and led her toward the bar. She tried to smile, but it hurt. She was grateful for the distraction, for the escape of noise and liquor and laughter.

"Come on, boy," she called to Radar, but he stayed where he was, watching her, tail low, as if he were worried about her.

"Forget it then," she said, a stabbing feeling low inside her. She was worried about herself, too.

This was better, though, she tried to tell herself. For a while there, she'd forgotten who she was. She was at the beach on vacation, dammit. She was a party girl. If she'd stuck with that, she wouldn't be fighting tears this minute.

This was a lesson, dammit, and she would learn it.

MATT STOOD ROOTED to the spot, his insides churning, his mind frozen, until Candy was out of sight. She was right *and* wrong, but it would take him a bit to sort out which was which. He shouldn't have offered her the job to make her feel better. She was right about that. That was bad for her and SyncUp and no way for a vice president to behave.

She was right that being together would change things at work. He was no good at secrets, how he felt about her would show. Ellie said he was transparent as glass.

Would staff respect him less? And what about Candy? Already, employees thought her wild. Would being with him help or hurt her reputation?

The affair had been irresponsible. He should have known better. He had an obligation to be discreet. He should be fired. He would have to resign. Not right away, of course, because he wouldn't strand Scott and he'd make sure Candy was in good shape first. She'd been so hurt about the team-leader issue.

He was suddenly exhausted by the whole thing. What was he doing standing here, his heart burning with loss? He was an idiot, dressed like some surfer dude, blinking to see through these stupid contacts. He needed peace and quiet, time online and his damn glasses back. If he'd stuck with who he was, none of this would have happened.

At his place, the quiet didn't help the way he'd expected it to. He missed Candy as if something had been cut out of him. He stayed clear of the bedroom where the sheets were tangled from all their lovemaking, but he could still smell her perfume everywhere.

He fought the urge to chase her down, kiss away their doubts, make love until it all made sense again.

What about when we break up? She'd said it as though it were inevitable, just part of the package. It angered him that she could be so casual about something that was so big to him.

That was the point, wasn't it? To Candy it was casual, not life-altering.

She was Heather all over again. Crazy fun, then the crash that hurt like hell. Maturity would not lessen his pain. How had he even thought that?

He'd been an idiot. He knew better. Stick to your strengths, don't take chances. If you had too much fun, there was hell to pay—like that Tsunami for Two he'd paid for with a hangover. He was paying again, all right. This time, the lesson would stick.

CANDY WOKE THE NEXT morning to a fuzzy brain and the sound of someone snoring. She turned her head and saw two big, sand-streaked feet sticking up from beneath the sheet.

Whoops. She whipped back the covers and found Carter asleep on his belly, stark naked, his head at the foot of her foldout bed.

Omigod. Had she? She looked down at herself, relieved she still wore her dress. She would have remembered sex, of course, regardless of how much alcohol she'd drunk. They'd had winner shots of tequila after they'd won the darts contest and she'd downed a blue martini to further numb her sadness.

As a result, her head was killing her, but she had no

regrets. She'd been pure party girl—danced on the bar, on a table, even on Carter's shoulders while he loped down the beach to burn off the booze. She'd laughed a lot. Whenever she reminded herself she was having a good time, anyway.

She peeked again at her snoring bedmate. What a golden male specimen he was. Normally, she'd wake him and screw his brains out.

But not today. Today, the idea was so wrong it made her feel queasy. She covered him up.

It'll be fine, she told herself. There would be plenty of Carters around when she was ready again. But Matts? Where would she find another Matt? Despair made her sink into the mattress. She wasn't sure she even wanted to get out of bed.

She heard steps on the stairs and looked up to see Sara descending in a beaded minidress—obviously from the night before. Her friend looked as miserable as Candy felt. Her eyes were red, her hair tangled.

When she caught sight of Candy in bed, she pointed at the feet and mouthed, "Matt?"

Candy shook her head, fingers to her lips, then motioned Sara toward the kitchen, where she would join her to talk. She didn't want to wake Carter—couldn't take his eager energy at the moment. *What do we do now? Huh? Huh?* He was the human version of Radar, always ready to play. And she was pretty sure sex would be his top-of-mind idea.

She climbed out of bed, sweaty and sandy, her dress a wrinkled mess and followed Sara to the kitchen, where she would make her hangover mix, though she knew it would take more than protein powder and B vitamins to ease her pain.

"What happened, Sara?"

"Never mind me. Who's that?" She pointed toward the bed.

"That's Carter. We hung out last night after…Matt and I broke up." The words hurt to say. "We won a bunch of points playing darts, though." Candy reached into her bodice for the voucher slip, which she handed to Sara.

"Forget the points," Sara said, tossing the paper on the counter. "Can you and Matt straighten things out?"

Tears welled in Candy's eyes and she could only shake her head.

"Oh, hon. I'm so sorry." Sara hugged her.

"It was impossible from the start and we both knew it." Candy tried to collect herself. "Listen, can I borrow your laptop?" She'd saved all her files on her key drive, so she could do some work, despite everything.

Sara hesitated. "I guess so. Sure. I'll leave it here." She turned, looking confused. "Look, I've gotta go…" She motioned toward the stairs, then headed off.

"Wait. What's wrong?" she whispered, but Sara waved her away. Something was upsetting her. Candy would find out once she'd taken her hangover cure.

Footsteps on the stairs made her look up to see Ellie barreling down to her. "Hey, girl! What happened to you two?"

Candy put her finger to her lips and motioned at the bed. Carter let out a loud snore, not bothered by the noise. Ellie tiptoed into the kitchen. "Sorry," she said.

"What's up? Hangover?" She nodded at the cure ingredients Candy was combining.

"Yeah."

"Poor Matt." Ellie nodded affectionately toward Carter's feet.

"That's not Matt, Ellie." She turned to her friend. "Matt and I broke up."

"No!" Ellie looked horrified. "Was it because I told Matt about the teams? I'm so sorry. I know better than getting into other people's lives too much. I—"

"No. It was not you, Ellie. Matt wouldn't even consider me for the team-leader spot. He doesn't respect me."

"Sure he does," Ellie said. "This is just a misunderstanding. Let me talk to him. I'll straighten this out."

"No, you won't. It's our problem. We should never have gotten involved. It was a mistake to bring work out here. It didn't change a thing."

"I'm so sorry, Candy," Ellie said. "It was my idea."

"You were just trying to help me, Ellie. At least now I know where I stand." She drank the mix she'd made.

"Do you want me to stick around today? Hang with you?"

"No. Go enjoy yourself. Enjoy Bill. I've got work to do."

"Work? Don't get crazy with all that now."

"I'm not. I'll be fine. I'm sorry I crapped out on the party events. At least I got the darts points."

"We'll be fine, don't worry," Ellie said.

"Maybe I'll try to draft the essay about why we deserve the time-share."

"How can you do that? Your heart is broken." Ellie's

face was so full of empathy, Candy feared she might cry. "You'll never want to come to Malibu again."

Very possible, but she pushed past that thought. "Of course I will. To be with you and Sara? We'll have fun no matter what our love lives are like, right?"

Ellie smiled. "That's true."

"So, there you go," she said, her heart aching in her chest. "The essay will be something fun to concentrate on."

"I hope so," Ellie said.

A moan from the bed drew their attention and Carter emerged, pulling the sheet around his body. She introduced him to Ellie and offered him some hangover cure.

She'd just walked Carter to the door and told him good-bye, when Sara came downstairs lugging her suitcase. It turned out she and Drew had quarreled—was last night bust-up night or what?—and she was ready to run home and bail out Uncle Spence with some crisis or other. Candy and Ellie managed to talk her into staying for the surf competition, at least.

Eventually, Candy was on her own again. She was headed for Sara's computer when there was a bang at the door.

She opened it to find Radar looking eagerly up at her, ready to play. "Sorry, guy. Better find Carter."

The dog didn't move.

"Don't you give up? I have to work." In fact, she looked forward to it. She intended to finish what she'd started, even if she left SyncUp because of the Matt fiasco. The one good thing about this trip was that she'd realized she was more capable than she'd thought she was.

For all her sorrow, this cheered her a little.

"Can't you tell I'm a new girl?" she asked the dog.

But Radar just whined. He'd played with her before and that was all he needed to know.

The truth hit her like a Frisbee in the forehead. People's perceptions of you had to do with them, too, not just you. To Radar, Candy was a playmate. At SyncUp, people saw her as a jokester. That wouldn't change, even if she did show more maturity and self-discipline. They wouldn't notice the subtle improvements she'd made in herself.

What about her family?

She pictured the Thanksgiving scene she'd envisioned—the beautiful table, gleaming crystal, festive china, the dense aromas swirling in the air—roast turkey, pumpkin spice, sage dressing. Her father carving the bird. Everyone laughing, drinking wine and making the usual jokes about the time their father burned the bird or when Candy made a rubber-band shooter out of the wishbone.

She would ding her glass with her fork, to start the gratitude circle, the fine crystal ringing so crisply her ears would sting. "I'd like to start," she would say, "since I have something special to be thankful for this year."

"What? You didn't bounce a check all year? You bought shares in Jose Cuervo?"

She'd fight down the laughter. "Nothing like that. I got a promotion. I'm the head of a product team. A manager."

There would be a happy outcry and congratulations, but it would be the equivalent of "That's nice, dear."

They'd go back to talking about big legal deals, politics at the firm, the plans to expand her parents' factory. And they'd smile at her as though she were their darling little girl.

Still.

That's who she was to them. Over time, they'd accept the changes in her, but it would be incremental. One promotion wouldn't alter a lifetime of experiences and expectations.

No, her family wouldn't be nearly as impressed as she wanted them to be.

The person she needed to impress was herself. The question was how she saw herself and her abilities.

She *was* proud of herself. She was good at what she did. She was creative and innovative and good with people and a hell of a lot of fun.

Matt had said she'd be bored as a product manager. He might be right. She would hate the meetings, for sure. And cracking the whip? Forget it. He was correct that she'd have trouble getting staff to take her seriously because of all the joking around she did—maybe she didn't want them to.

She liked who she was. She didn't need to be a manager to be successful. But she wanted something more, some advancement. What about owning her own agency? The idea had come up a couple of times on the trip. Sara and Ellie had talked about it. Claudia and her business group had tried to hire her. She'd planned to do that eventually. Why not now? Or soon, anyway?

She might even get SyncUp as a client. She knew Scott hired outside consultants from time to time. Hell, she'd be better than the last guy they used. If Matt had meant what he'd said about wanting her for all his teams. Of course he did. The man was as honest as sunrise.

Her head began to throb, but in a good way this time. She'd wasted time trying to be someone she wasn't. She was a girl who mixed work and play. And there was nothing wrong with that. The relief made her whole body feel shot through with light.

And she owed it, in part, to Matt. Painful as it was, he'd helped her see her strengths. He *knew* her.

For all their differences, he *got* her. She felt appreciated, accepted, valued by him for all she was, not all she thought she should be.

That was important and her eyes filled with tears of gratitude. She would thank him. But first she would sketch out some ideas for her new agency. What would she call it?

Candy Can? Calder Creative? Yeah, that sounded very good.

The idea made her smile and filled her with fire. She'd have something to report at Thanksgiving, after all. Even if all she got was a pat on her head for it, she'd know the truth. Candy Calder was going places.

15

MATT SAT AT HIS computer staring at his favorite tech e-zine, not caring one whit about malevolent bots or the latest on data farming.

He'd written out a possible team chart, but he kept worrying about where Candy would fit best and what if she quit?

He balled up the chart and tossed it across the room into his upside-down ball cap. Two points! Candy would make up rules for this, turn it into an office event.

She made everything fun. They needed her at SyncUp, for morale reasons if nothing else. If this thing between them chased her away, he'd never forgive himself.

He heard a sound on his porch and went to the door. There was Radar with that Frisbee of his. The dog nosed his way inside and galloped from room to room, carrying the Frisbee, searching for something. Or someone. When he returned, his doggie face held an obvious question: *Where's Candy?*

"She's not here, pal, but I'll play." He reached for the Frisbee, but the dog backed off, disappointed, then turned and trotted away.

He knew exactly how the dog felt. Candy opened all

the windows and doors and let the sun in. She'd helped him see what he'd been missing.

He needed her in his life, dammit. If she would have him. He'd have to figure out how to make things right for her at SyncUp. He could quit, like he'd thought earlier. SyncUp was a great company and he'd made VP, but he'd moved before. To keep Candy in his life, he'd do anything.

Anything.

That realization made something shift inside him. He'd changed. He'd always done what was sensible, conservative, expected. What had Candy asked him: Did he act out of obligation or joy? He'd never thought about it before. He considered joy a luxury, beginning as a kid when he'd had to take care of his mother and sister. That was years ago and his family was fine. He had no further obligation to them.

He could do what gave him joy. And being with Candy did that. In spades. What a gift it was to have one person mean everything to him. One person whose laughter made his heart light, his life sweet.

One woman he wanted to help and be helped by. She got him out of his head, shook him out of the dull grind of every day that he found so comforting, but which also closed him away from new ideas and experiences. Adventures.

He needed Candy in his life.

And he could only hope that Candy needed him, too. There was only one way to find out.

A SMALL THUD AGAINST the screen door made Candy look up. Her neck ached and her bottom was numb from sitting at the computer so long. She'd been sketching out a business plan for Calder Creative and hadn't noticed the time going by. Nothing was more enthralling than planning your future, it seemed. It would take months to enact the change, she knew, but each moment that passed made her more sure this was the right thing to do.

She couldn't wait to talk to Matt about it. She hoped he'd be interested in hiring her as a consultant.

More importantly, she hoped he'd still want to be with her. Once she'd figured out what she wanted for her career, once she'd separated the promotion disappointment from her feelings for Matt, she realized she wanted to be with him. She wanted to be a couple, to give their feelings a chance to grow.

She thought they could help each other. He would be her safe haven and she would make sure he didn't miss life's little side trips.

At the door, she found Radar nudging the screen to get her attention. When he saw her, he wagged his whole body.

"You think it's time for a break, huh?" She smiled. She had been sitting still too long and she *was* at the beach, after all.

On the porch, her cell phone rang. She had it in her pocket, expecting a call back from SyncUp over a question she'd had. She dug it out of her capris, but, just like the first day, it slid from her fingers to the porch.

Radar nabbed it and ran off.

"Wait!" she said, then ran after him toward the water, where she noticed a man stood, bare-chested, waves foaming at his feet, a phone at his ear.

It was Matt. He wore his new swim trunks and his old glasses. Radar galloped up to him, her phone in his mouth, as if Matt had asked him to fetch it.

Candy's heart lifted and she laughed and joined them. "Radar grabbed my phone again," she said.

"I see that." He looked down at the dog, who was backing away, teasing them into another game of keep-away.

"It's me calling." He pointed at his phone, then closed it and shoved it into the flapped pocket of his trunks. "I wanted to know if you could come out and play with me." He smiled his wry half-smile.

"I'd love to," she said, her heart filling up and spilling over.

"I mean *for the rest of our lives*," he said, his voice husky with emotion. His eyes shone at her, blue and clear as the Malibu sky, the glasses no barrier at all.

She felt tears spring to her eyes. "I'd love to try that." More than anything she'd ever wanted in her life.

"I'm glad. I have so much to say. I don't know where to begin."

"How about with getting my phone before Radar chews it up?" She lunged for the dog, who feinted joyfully to the left.

They were soon playing the phone game again with Radar, laughing and lunging, missing and falling until finally, Candy tackled Radar and Matt pried away the phone.

They both lay on the sand.

Radar raced away, as if he'd achieved his goal.

Maybe he had.

They sat up and Matt brushed sand from her cheek.

"I'm always a mess around you," she said.

"You're always perfect around me. Whether you've got margarita on your chin, sand on your cheek or whipped cream on your nose. Whether you're grinning at me or giving me hell. You're just what I need. Playful and smart and stubborn and fierce. However you are, that's fine with me."

"You're what I need, too, Matt. I like that you're steady, that you make me feel secure and safe. I like how you focus and how serious you are."

"I can be boring, I'll warn you."

"We'll work on that," she teased. "Shake things up a little. Within reason."

"I can deal with that."

"I love that you *get* me. In some ways better than I get myself. You were right that being a team leader isn't for me."

"Really? You agree?"

"I was hurt at first. The promotion seemed like proof that I was a success, that you respected me."

"I do respect you. You're amazing. You could do anything you set your mind to, but—"

"But if it makes me miserable, what's the point? That's what I need from you—to be my reality check."

"And I need you to get me out of my rut, make me look up."

"And see the parasail? Yeah. I think we can be good for each other." She was so happy she thought her heart might burst.

"We have to deal with SyncUp." Matt took on his

cut-to-the-chase look. "Being your boss would be tricky, so the best thing will be for me to resign. As soon as it's feasible."

"You can't resign. You just made VP." She was so touched. The man was ready to toss his carefully constructed career plan out of love for her. "I'm going to quit."

"You can't quit. SyncUp needs you, Candy."

"It *can* have me. As a consultant. How's that? I think I want to start my own agency. It's been in the back of my mind for down the line, but why not now? Or in the next year anyway. I have the skills and the drive. It's the right next step, I think. I've already worked up some ideas."

"Are you sure?" He studied her. "Because I'd love to have you as a consultant. That way you could work with all the teams. Depending on our budget, of course."

She smiled. "Sure. I'd like your thoughts on my rates, too. I've got some ideas drafted. Come and see." She started to get up, but Matt caught her hand and tugged her onto his lap. "You and your working vacation. Could you hold off a bit? I'm going to have to teach you how to relax."

She laughed and wrapped her arms around him and tilted her face for a kiss. Her cheek bumped his glasses, so she pulled them off. "These are a pain." She studied them, then looked at him. "So the makeover was a bust?"

"Not entirely. I like my glasses. And forget hair gel. But some of the changes were good. I sang karaoke, did the limbo, drank too much blue liqueur and, hell, was freak danced upon. That was all good. I needed that."

"So you're Matt, version 1.5, instead of 2.0?"

"Exactly," he said, standing and reaching to lift her into his arms.

"What do you have in mind?"

"Mmm. I need a few more networking tips, don't you think?" He started toward his beach house, carrying her tight against his chest.

Radar woofed, running up to them.

"Check with us later, pal," Matt said. "We've got some catching up to do."

Candy smiled down at the eager retriever. "We need a dog, don't you think? To remind us to come out and play?"

"I think all we need is each other."

She realized he was right. They'd been made over by love, seeing each other with new eyes, learning from each other and teaching each other, too.

Right now, she couldn't wait to get naked and let the lessons begin.

* * * * *

Don't miss the next book in the
SEX ON THE BEACH *series!*
Look for Shock Waves *by Colleen Collins,*
coming in July 2008 from Blaze®!

Wait!

The excitement's not over yet!!!

*Theo Angelis still has an adventure – and a very
sexy woman – waiting for him. And he's not
prepared for either one of them…*

Don't miss The Defender, *available next month.*

Here's a sneak peek…

The Defender

by

Cara Summers

THEO FLOATED ON HIS BACK in the water, enjoying the gentle movement of the waves. Above him the moon and stars crowded the clear night sky. He'd lost track of the number of laps he'd swum, but even though his muscles were weak, his mind relaxed, he hadn't been able to get Sadie Oliver out of his mind. Sooner or later, he was going to have to figure out why.

He was about to climb onto the dock when the silence was broken by a sharp, staccato knocking sound. Then he heard Bob hit the screen door. Grabbing the dock with one hand, Theo glanced toward the shore. He couldn't imagine either Kit or Nik knocking on the cabin door. From the angle he was at a tree blocked his view, but he clearly heard Bob bark and launch himself at the door again.

Bob was not the best watchdog. In spite of his size, the dog had the people-loving instincts of a golden retriever and viewed any stranger as a possible source of petting or food and hopefully both.

Staying very still in the water, Theo waited and a moment later saw a figure move around the side of the cabin. He got a quick impression of height—the build was more slender than either of his brothers. He'd left the light on in his bedroom, and when the figure turned to face the window, he had a clear view of a silhouette in profile. Female, he thought. The light wasn't strong enough for him to see her features, but he made out that she was wearing a skirt.

Annoyance and frustration streamed through him. Following the arrest of his stalker, he'd convinced the group of women who'd been attending his trials for the past few months to stop. And they had. For the last two months, he'd thought that he'd gotten his life back to normal.

But he couldn't think of another reason why a woman would have come all this way to track him down at midnight. He wasn't dating anyone. And this woman was too tall to be his sister Philly. Besides, Philly would have walked right in. She and Bob were old friends.

The figure moved back toward the front of the cabin, her knock louder this time. He thought of calling out to her, but didn't. Instead, moving quietly, he swam toward shore, and once he got his feet beneath him, he walked slowly out of the water. He was still twenty yards away when he saw her open the screen door and walk in. He had to give her points for courage. Bob might be a pushover, but he did have that size thing going for him. To his surprise, he saw her crouch down and speak to the dog, but the sound of the waves behind him muffled her words. Okay, so she had guts and she liked big dogs. But she was still in a place she had no business being. Technically, she was breaking and entering.

She'd already disappeared into the cabin by the time he reached it. Carefully, he opened the porch door and turned sideways to slip in before the hinge creaked.

She'd left the inner door to the cabin open. In the darkness of the kitchen, he could only make out her silhouette as she stood peering out the window in the direction of the lake.

Annoyance streamed through him again. Bold as brass, he thought. Not only had she followed him out here to a place that he'd always considered a refuge, but she'd walked right in. It didn't help his mood one bit that Bob was sitting at her feet, beating his tail against the floor, evidently pleased as punch at the new visitor. At the very least, Theo figured he owed her a good scare.

He flipped on the light. "What the hell do you think—"

She wirled and her scream blocked the rest of his sentence.

"Sadie?" Since he hadn't been able to get her out of his mind while he was swimming, his first thought was that he'd conjured her up. His second was that in another moment she was going to slip right to the floor. Cursing himself, he strode to her. She'd gone pale as the moonlight on the water. "Are you all right?"

Stupid question when he could see that she was anything but. Taking her arm, he eased her into one of the chairs at the table. Then he moved to the refrigerator, retrieved the bottle of wine he'd opened earlier and filled a glass. She was still trembling when he set it in front of her, so he took the chair next to hers and covered her hand with his to help her lift the glass.

She took a sip and swallowed. Then their eyes met and held over the rim of the glass. He was touching only her hand, and yet there was that intensity, that same connection he'd felt when he'd clasped her hand in the courtroom. Suddenly, Theo knew. Not merely that their paths would cross again, but that she was the *one,* the one woman for him.

No. Panic shot up his spine, and nerves knotted in his abdomen. He wasn't ready. He forced himself to take a deep breath as he reminded himself that he still had a choice. The Fates only presented choices.

But as Sadie lifted the glass for another sip, he didn't remove his hand from hers, and he couldn't seem to take his eyes off her. Her lips were parted and moist from the wine. He very badly wanted to taste that mouth. Even as lust curled into a tight hot fist in his stomach, he let his hand drop and eased himself back in his chair. He had to get away before…

Rising, he strode toward the adjoining hallway. "Drink the wine while I change. then you can tell me why you're here."

SADIE LET OUT THE BREATH she hadn't even been aware she was holding and barely kept the wineglass from slipping out of her hand. Very carefully, she set it on the table. Her head was still foggy, still spinning. And it wasn't merely because he'd scared her. It was because he'd touched her again. All he'd meant to do was steady the wineglass, just as all he'd done in that courtroom was shake her hand.

How was it that each time he put a hand on her, even in the most casual of ways, it was as if he'd touched her all over?

She pressed her fingers to her temples, willing her mind to clear and her thoughts to settle. When she'd whirled to see him standing in the doorway, he hadn't looked like the Theo Angelis she'd seen in court. He'd looked larger than life, like some god from the sea, his dark hair slicked back, those even darker eyes with that hint of danger. And all that damp, tanned skin. Even now, she was astonished at how much she wanted to touch him, to taste him. More than that, she wanted to devour him.

No man had ever affected her this way. With hands that trembled, she reached for her wine and took another swallow.

She was overreacting. There were too many emotions pounding at her—Roman, Juliana, the walk through the woods. She had to get a grip. She'd come here to ask Kit Angelis to help her. She couldn't afford to fall apart.

"I'm sorry I gave you a scare."

Startled, she whirled in her chair to watch Theo pour himself a glass of wine. Then he reached into the refrigerator and pulled out a plate of cheese. He was wearing old jeans that had faded at the seams and hem and an equally ancient T-shirt. The general rattiness of the clothes surprised her. Theo had always been so impeccably dressed in his court appearances.

"These are my lucky fishing clothes."

Sadie's gaze flew to his face. Could he read her mind? Was she that transparent to him?

His lips curved as he set the plate of cheese between them and sank into a chair. "Whenever I wear them, I catch the biggest fish. My brothers are hoping that one day soon the cloth will disintegrate and fall off me."

In her mind, Sadie pictured them doing just that— first the T-shirt, the jeans… Was he wearing briefs beneath them? As heat pooled in her center, Sadie ruthlessly focused. She was not going to get anywhere if she continued to imagine Theo Angelis naked.

* * * * *

FREE!
2 Books
and a surprise gift!

We would like to take this opportunity to thank you for reading this Mills & Boon® book by offering you the chance to take TWO more specially selected titles from the Blaze® series absolutely FREE! We're also making this offer to introduce you to the benefits of the Mills & Boon® Reader Service™—

- ★ FREE home delivery
- ★ FREE gifts and competitions
- ★ FREE monthly Newsletter
- ★ Exclusive Reader Service offers
- ★ Books available before they're in the shops

Accepting these FREE books and gift places you under no obligation to buy, you may cancel at any time, even after receiving your free shipment. Simply complete your details below and return the entire page to the address below. You don't even need a stamp!

YES! Please send me 2 free Blaze books and a surprise gift. I understand that unless you hear from me, I will receive 4 superb new titles every month for just £3.15 each, postage and packing free. I am under no obligation to purchase any books and may cancel my subscription at any time. The free books and gift will be mine to keep in any case.

K8ZEF

Ms/Mrs/Miss/Mr ....Initials ....
BLOCK CAPITALS PLEASE
Surname ....
Address ....

....

....Postcode ....

Send this whole page to:
UK: FREEPOST CN81, Croydon, CR9 3WZ